Nicole Brossard
translated by
Susanne de Lotbinière-Harwood

Fences in Breathing

Coach House Books | Toronto

First English edition. Originally published in French as *La capture du sombre* by Leméac Éditeur, 2007.

Translated with the support of the Canada Council for the Arts Translation program. Published with the generous assistance of the Canada Council for the Arts and the Ontario Arts Council. Coach House Books also acknowledges the support of the Government of Ontario through the Ontario Book Publishing Tax Credit and the Government of Canada through the Book Publishing Industry Development Program.

LIBRARY AND ARCHIVES CANADA CATALOGUING IN PUBLICATION

Brossard, Nicole, 1943-
[Capture du sombre. English]
 Fences in breathing / Nicole Brossard ; translated by Susanne de Lotbinière-Harwood.

Translation of: La capture du sombre.
ISBN 978-1-55245-213-4

 I. Lotbinière-Harwood, Susanne de II. Title. III. Title: Capture du sombre. English.

PS8503.R7C3613 2009   C843'.54   C2009-901301-0

§

The dark suspends everything. There is nothing that can,
in the dark, become true.

Alessandro Baricco

I often check my watch. Sometimes, on the luminous back of its face, I catch the reflection of my eyes. Since yesterday, something has slipped into my thoughts that has altered the course of time in such a way that, for reasons still unknown to me, I feel like slowly writing a book in a language other than my own. A way of avoiding short-circuits in my mother tongue, perhaps also of fleeing. Like a foreigner, I want to dive into the landscape of a temporary world where meaning parts meaning as I move through it. I am writing this book also as a way of not being soft and of seeing the horizon of fires heading our way.

I am everywhere I am. I am here to understand and to escape. I have put some distance between my mother tongue and reality. I am valiantly trying to imagine how pleasures and joys, fears and frights, can be built in a language not at all familiar. I am trying most of all to understand how, with a vertical body, it is possible to impale the real at the same speed as fiction. Then, without falling apart, I let immensity softly softly drop its Nordic melancholy blueness upon my shoulders.

All around me, the vast kingdom of time past forces me to coexist with words unknown, words so harsh I hesitate to utter them, because speaking what one harbours makes a cold meal of the story of our very sincere lives.

I am constantly straining to keep urging life forward, that luminous and fascinating prey, and then I stay still for days at a time, surrounded by words and midnight graves. This time of urgency and vertigo forces me to heed what I call the *torment of grammar fast turning around into abyss.* That's how it is.

I will do what it takes to understand, but I'll need to streamline, to display the dark, embrace it, carve up its soul, in full daylight if need be.

Many before me have chosen to write in a language other than the one given them in childhood. Each time, the wind kept them suspended over a fertile void, bringing them neither farther from nor closer to the place where spirited children thirst to name everything. The world is always ready to seize our joys and pains and turn them into a landscape of its own. That world is perhaps nameless, unwritten, swallowed just in time by a number of dawns and dusks unappeased by languor and by reason.

Years went by and never did I feel the gloom settle into my daily gestures. Nothing at the root of my thoughts made it possible to foresee a darkening that was not just periodic and minor. Then one day, barely perceptible in the landscape, a little amoeba-shaped birthmark, an obscuring of houses, trees, passersby, women and their children. A feeling of both menace and tenderness, as sometimes happens while writing a biography, or when holding the hand of a stranger.

There is black on the horizon, a surface that does not reflect light and steals space from the very precious volume of life that is a child's arms, the foliage of tall, feathery trees, the turquoise surface of the water at the foot of glaciers. In my language, I have exhausted the vocabulary that would have allowed me to name that intriguing, approaching black: raven, vulture, feline, the black of volcanic sand, of marble, of ink and soot, of leather, of cassocks, of niqab and chador, and of burnt corpse. I need other words for this darkness of nature and civilization now encroaching.

When travelling, I still occasionally dream, but with ever smaller images, hard to pinpoint, like miniatures composed of countless illegible letters, assembled on a tenuous surface as if a world were about to be erased, but one whose disappearance remains as yet unthinkable.

I am everywhere I am. Nowadays, a lot of words catch fire in my dreams, relieving me neither of my mother tongue nor of the other one already altering my thoughts, I know, making me even more despondent than I was.

Something silent goes through me when I think of the foreign language. Like on the day I met with a friend at a restaurant where meals were served and eaten in total darkness. Keeping your eyes closed or open made no difference. Our every word and gesture sank into a blackness both opaque and nameless that I chose to describe as friendly because it presented itself like a playful invention for refining the senses. There was nothing frightening about that blackness; it was part of a realm that had so far escaped my sensory experience. Like everybody, I'd gotten used to the semi-darkness of cities and believed it offered a joyful alternative to the night. That day, I had to learn to breathe deeply, to eliminate those little fences of resistance that, in normal circumstances, take my breath away and make me paw the ground with desire and anguish.

Nobody seeks darkness, nobody enjoys seeing the times darken. I know nothing of the dark. Then suddenly it appears, a feline finding its spot in the daily life of beliefs. Now it is my turn to go toward it, to get closer and search its soul with the invisible part of my own, which, since yesterday, has started to come alive in a foreign language.

SKETCHBOOK

I don't believe in events enough to write stories.

Joë Bousquet

For a few days now I've been living at the château and sleeping in a canopy bed. In truth it's a theatre, with curtain, dais, valance, festoons, fringes and tassels that make me anxious. All this leaves me feeling disoriented and propels me into thinking about a cycle of birth, death and procreation. Arena of the old masters, the poster bed shelters frightening rituals. Certainly the bed is deeply ridiculous, but this does not make it insignificant. It acts as memory by recalling the obligation of continuity and legacy so that, *bang*, blood continues to flow in the name of lineage and survival. In my language, *royal bed* and *one-night stand* designate common places to discuss reproduction. At the château, time has run in a straight line, carefully smoothing sharp edges, bad tempers, affronts and exchanges, and even the cold, which, when it penetrates too deep into flesh, raises it just enough to cause fears and shivers. The room is large and only the two small side tables from the

1950s calm me down a little. Tatiana must have bought them after acquiring the château. In the afternoon, I walk in the rose garden. Sometimes I smoke a cigarette. In the distance, the mountains draw curves in the paleness of the day. I think about the words I'd like to use but cannot be said in my language. Wind, always, shakes the roses.

§

While soaping her mother's back, Laure talks to her slowly, softly. The sponge is soft. When she makes a fist, her hand wraps around it completely, then the sponge springs back to its original shape, a dishevelled little animal. Laure, the cool urban lawyer, has settled in the village among forgotten childhood girlfriends and strangers who, like her, work for a multinational or a government, or for their own interests. Summer evenings, she can be seen walking in the little wood or sitting in the garden, a cigarette in one hand, a glass of white wine in the other. By day, after helping her mother with her morning routine, she dives into an analysis of every word in the Patriot Act. Laure the urbanite can remain thus for hours, poring over texts that make the law; then, at the end of the day, she goes back to her mother, prepares her meal, bathes her, fixes her hair, kisses her and bids goodnight to this woman from whose womb she emerged forty years ago like a nice cliché.

§

Every morning around eight o'clock, bells ring. A few strikes of the gong and the sky lights up, starts to move, trembles. I can barely control my excitement about fully comparing, for example, the birds' discreet song with the wind's whistling through the leaves. The air is fresh on my skin. A plane flies by in the distance. I don't see it; only its shipwreck sound reaches me. Since September 11, planes are bombs, *trompe l'oeil* tombs in the sky, and I have lost some of that happiness, which, while it was never quite tranquility, nonetheless left me with joy deep in my soul, certain that the world and the meaning of my life could not so readily fall apart. Ever since then, words can no longer rise to the task of consolation. So I throw myself upon *village* and *château*, still making very sure to not get too estranged from the word *literature*. This one I keep at the core of my silence, that beautiful lush space suspended over the void.

§

Today, as he heads to the post office, Charles's step is a worried one. A nervousness in the movement of the arms, short steps and a sharp gleam in his eye. Charles, the woodworker, the sculptor, the sketch artist who for twenty years has amassed objects whose function, he says, is to show what men are capable of: inkwells, astrolabes, globes, pens, chandeliers, perfume atomizers, chairs named after kings and emperors, old Remingtons and Olivettis. In the last five years, his workshop has also been filling up with first-generation cellphones and laptops. Empty Southern Comfort bottles stand side by side with beautiful old-fashioned crystal carafes and the Lilliputian armoires he has sculpted from oak and whimsy. The man spends his time between the workshop and the post office, where he always has forms to fill out. It's a five-minute walk to the post office. The view of the valley is magnificent: vineyards, fields of sunflowers and corn unfurling a mix of yellow, brown and green that floods the gaze with a stream of light likely to penetrate the soul with the speed of a fox. Today Charles is afraid. His left hand, covered in scars, trembles when he is close to June. In my language, I can see the trembling very clearly. Now, I don't know more than that. June is beautiful in both languages.

§

I arrived at the château on the Wednesday preceding the incident. I was coming to meet Tatiana Beaujeu Lehmann, retired publisher. A woman still sprightly, generous, who single-handedly carried an entire body of literature at a time when it seemed about to give way to another one, produced in a language so foreign that even today nobody seems to have figured out what was at stake. In time, the other literature nevertheless won out. So Tatiana Beaujeu sold her publishing house and ended all dealings with most of the people who surrounded her with their half-truths. For half-truths had become common currency to explain reality, as if everything had the same value, *glass half full, glass half empty* acting as an example now to exalt the empty part, now to praise the full part. One never said *half-lie*, never. Nevertheless, people swallowed everything they could from the little goblet of lies. Half-truths flew off in one direction, then, having morphed into rumour, gossip and *narrative* lethal to all men and women who continued to dream of a better world, flew back like a poisoned arrow straight at the heart of their thoughts.

§

Yes, his hand was trembling. The foreign woman's gaze drifted over his fingers, then he felt it wrap round his wrist. At that precise moment, Charles's hand began to tremble. Even after holding his hand around the handle of a heavy hammer for a long time or after carving the shape of his solitude a thousand times into the belly of a tree, he had never trembled. No, that had never happened, and now it started to at the very moment June spoke to him to enquire about his sister, who so craved to live in the Svalbard archipelago in northern Norway. Suddenly there was a whirlwind of triangles in which he distinguished the faces of June and his sister, then another triangle formed with the silhouettes of Laure and the foreign woman. Both times he thought he saw his own shadow in the midst. But it was not him, he knew it was not him. Now his hand was no longer trembling, and he entered the post office. 'What a wind!' the employee said while looking for a form in the bottom drawer of a desk. 'What a wind!' Charles repeated with a worried look.

§

The château is home to Tatiana and her personal secretary, who takes care of everything, including the letter, received six months ago, inviting me to stay at the château in exchange for a few conversations and reflections on the current state of the world. 'Fewer and fewer people will go to libraries in search of their dignity,' said Tatiana. 'I need all this explained to me.' The publisher had bought the château in the middle of the twentieth century. There are a thousand and one little reminders of America in the fifties: drinking gin, rye and whisky, as people did over there back then, must have occurred a lot here as well. The staircase and the bedroom floors are covered in thick white carpet always just about to turn from pearl to yellow, from yellow to the grey in the air. On each side of the bed, a little table like those once found in the rooms of great hotels. When I stretch out my arm, I can press a series of buttons, launch an opera aria or a jazz tune, summon an imaginary employee via intercom, set the alarm or light the bed. It was the beginning of a new era, and owning a château did not prevent one from decorating it American-style. Tatiana is from another time, she represents what was most brilliant, generous and liberal in a bygone world fuelled by the pleasure of books, by socialism, by the soothing silence of leisurely strolls and the joys of conversation. At eighty-five, Tatiana has a sharpness of mind that can cut through umbilical cords and black thoughts with a single reply. To me, Tatiana speaks only about literature and writers she has known. Never about war, nor the Great Depression, nor the Holocaust, nor about science. But she leaves me free to talk about Québec's Quiet Revolution and about September 11. And every time this happens, I am surprised that the fact that she is all at once Jewish and Russian, a Québécoise and a New Yorker, helps me to compose in the foreign tongue.

§

Laure moves the sponge with care. From top to bottom, three times along each vertebra, then her hand makes a half-turn and heads for the left shoulder, over the nape of the neck and down again by the right shoulder, where the shoulder blade makes a slight bump, then everything becomes smooth. She repeats the same trajectory twice for each shoulder, quite naturally dipping the sponge into the bathwater once she reaches the kidney area. The most difficult part is always the breasts and belly. Not because of their lack of muscle tone, but because Laure's imagination travels at the speed of light. So that whenever she lightly touches that white soft mass of the belly, it is like caressing a child's cheek. A vanilla smell wafts through the damp air, reminiscent of the one in Las Vegas casinos, a pervasive scent of candy.

§

In the foreign language, I am unable to correctly assess the proximity of beings around me. Nor am I able to measure the distance that separates us. Proximity remains difficult for me to comprehend. A mysterious choreography brings us so fervently close to certain beings and imperceptibly distances us from others. Grasping the other in oneself always puts language to the test. Tatiana and I often talk about the little miracles of meaning fostered by intimate confidential exchanges, though we do not give in to them. The other evening, I'm not quite sure how, I ended up describing some of Mark Rothko's untitled paintings, while insisting on the magic found in the series by Aurélie Nemours entitled *Structure du silence*. Without realizing it, I may have put too much emphasis on Rothko's suicide. As she turned to gaze out the window overlooking the garden, Tatiana asked me to pour her a bit of sherry. She waited until I stopped talking before announcing that tomorrow we would go walking on the chemin du Signal. 'From up there you'll get a better view of the lake and the mountains. For the moment, why not just keep to the pleasure of imagining that the times have no effect on us. Let's allow the newspapers to pile up on the living-room table.'

§

On her way to the post office, June thinks of Kim's inevitable departure. She might have the time to install some new software on Kim's computer. Kim has long dreamt of leaving the village, of no longer seeing her brother. 'He's started a series of armoires that send chills down my spine. I need to travel to the north, to be reborn as a silhouette in space, without landmarks. I want day and night, the entire surface of their twenty-four hours, in my eyes, in my body. It doesn't matter to me what I become in that boundless Far North!' June might leave with Kim.

§

Is there any way of concluding with certainty that the world has changed? In five, ten years from now, what will my stay at the château come to mean? I see few people. I follow Tatiana's advice: don't read the newspapers, don't turn on the TV, hidden behind a folding screen as if it were the château's disgrace. Seeing no one does me good, but it's best, I do believe, to love your neighbour. Our worlds are made of a few words, a few images and an energy that each of us always shapes the same way, regardless of its intensity. In the foreign tongue, I occasionally don't finish my sentences. I feel ashamed when this happens. Yesterday Tatiana had me read an article entitled 'Could humans coexist, form a community in a society that had a legislative system but no code of ethics?' The question leaves me thinking. Therein lies a fissure in meaning that distresses me, that threatens my integrity, so I prefer to believe that in the end, life will once again win out, rough, warm. Half truth, half fiction.

§

As usual, the café is empty. An unknown woman is sitting at the back of the room. She is writing or taking notes, who knows. The day is so warm and green, one could die of pleasure under the shade of the great trees that Charles still keeps wanting to cut down to make into sculptures. In the far distance, the mountains, and sometimes the great white jet of precious water that, they say, brings the city good fortune. The lake is glassy and untroubled. The day cleanses the slow dust that has accumulated hour after hour.

§

On the wall of my room, four photographs of Tatiana. She must have been ten years old. The era is easy to recognize because back then there was only one way of framing faces. All the girls' hair was cut in the same style, with short bangs exposing the eyes and forehead. Tatiana seemed different because in her gaze one could easily imagine Red Square covered in snow, a bygone Russia of forests and wild mythologies. Tatiana was from a time that filled lives with massacres and suffering so vivid they cannot be forgotten. But history was repeating itself and, yes, Tatiana would say once again, 'A massacre, my dear, is when there are corpses in a field, on a road or in a school, and you can't distinguish the faces from the arms and legs. A massacre, my dear, is man-made cock-and-bull that whips victims around willy-nilly in the wind, and then harder still. Afterwards, you have to trudge through the muddy fields, wiping the blood from the uteruses of women and from children's cheeks.'

§

It is through prose that the world is driven to creating assets; through poetry, it changes and reconnects with the living. I tire quickly when writing in another language. I still don't know where to properly place the silences. I cheat constantly. Something escapes me. Tires me out. Makes me flee. This morning I went to the post office. I rarely run into anyone at this hour, but I noticed a man talking with a woman. He was holding her left hand strangely in his right, a bit like someone wounded who, in order to shield himself from an unfortunate blow, shrivels up into himself, overwhelmed by an invisible burden. The woman seemed rather joyful and, as I watched her talking with the man, I thought for a moment that she could not see him. That he was a shadow, a tautological presence. My eyes met the woman's. The wind was blowing hard. My eyes watered like in winter.

§

Images come up, one after another, like slides in a carousel or like in a graphic novel without the words. Just faces looming up from urban landscapes or science-fiction. June sees them coming, spreads them out, reorganizes them in an endless flow of profiles and close-ups that act as sites of memory and of future. Since her childhood, everything in her has played out like in the movies. Her family is a film crew, the house a film set with moments of sober silence, or of eating and drinking and laughter, notebooks scattered all over the table. June owns the Videoreal shop. For the last three years, she has been renting out old movies and some recent releases. She refuses to stock soft or hard porn. What this costs her in terms of business she makes up for with the younger clientele who love to engage in discussion and leave the store with *Citizen Kane*, *The Deer Hunter*, *Death in Venice*, *Matrix* or *Star Trek*. An entire generation thus navigates between past and future without side-stepping the all-powerful present. June is a fanatic for the present, which, in her view, tempers the pain of living, protects from ghosts and counters mirages. To her, everything is a pretext for the pleasure of now: lighting a cigarette, watching a movie, stretching out in the sun, reading or not really reading, kissing on the lips. June claims to be happy because she does not hesitate to transform her pain into a character capable of playing many roles. 'Pain, come over here. Pain, go over there,' she tells herself, whenever she feels the urge to stage what she refers to as the most exhilarating moments of her existence.

§

Half past midnight, the house is silent. On the kitchen table, Laure Ravin has spread magazines, newspapers, two photo albums, all dated September 2001. She slowly turns the pages, hypnotized by everything she sees and does not really see. Here, an enormous fireball in a blue sky gorged with immensity. Here again, debris like so many tiny white paper airplanes floating in the foreground of a tall tower. Already ruins, already autumn and steel, shredded. Everywhere, a fire gnaws at the building and devours the things of life: photographs of children, coffee cup, pen, an Anatolian carpet, a pleasing painting. Everywhere, books, operating manuals, bills, contracts, printers, cellphones and BlackBerrys, ID cards, twenty-dollar bills, painkillers, all of this suddenly becomes nothing. Some say this is hell, some say this is war. Human forms halfway between bodies and chimeras gesticulating in front of windows. Torso, shoulder, white shirt, here a man, arms glued to his side, one leg bent at a 45-degree angle, freefalls headfirst to his death. The sun has disappeared. A woman wearing a pearl necklace is covered in ashes from head to toe. Everywhere, ghosts in business suits walk through the darkness of the great fog of civilization.

§

Sometimes I catch Tatiana looking at her collection of watches. A hundred or so timepieces, antique and modern, with their white gold, their bright silver, assembled over the years since the purchase of the château: bassine-cased watches with astronomical indicators or enamelled covers, watches with tactile hour indicators, pendant watches, hunting-cased watches, dress watches, aviators' wrist-watches, ladies' bracelet watches, gentlemen's watches. She touches them, rewinds the ones whose mechanisms she is familiar with, marvels, tries to imagine the why of so much research, of such refinement and beauty. All these wheels, all these bridges, these screws, these pins, these hands, these springs, assembled to tempt us into a fascination with time. Once a year, Tatiana goes into town to see the mother of all complication watches, the Calibre 89, which, in addition to showing mean sidereal time and incorporating the Gregorian calendar, is adorned with a celestial chart representing the Milky Way and making it possible to distinguish 2,800 northern-hemisphere stars. And further complications still, about which she cannot stop dreaming.

§

The workshop is cluttered, dark like a sentence between two wounds. Here and there, tools, hammers, pliers, nails and picks, all the colour of rust or the grey of time passing by. Dust of dust and dust of scrap metal, sawdust, blond and brown wood chips that stick to your soles when you enter. Charles is sitting on his cracked leather sofa the colour of an old asphalt road. The tobacco smell of three generations of great drinkers and talkers has permeated the sofa. Charles has known them all, because the writers who once regularly visited the château liked him. Some bought his wood carvings, light enough to be carried all around the world; to others he gave those little boxes that look like drawers that he has never stopped reproducing, hoping someday, in a ritual gesture, to sow them at the bottom of the lake. With the men, he drank and talked about what made blood rush to his head. Few women visited him, but those who did enjoyed sitting on the sofa, smoking. When they asked too many questions about his work, Charles got a worried look on his face. When the woman did not grasp quickly enough that he was in pain, his eyes darkened. He enjoyed that moment when he could sense himself being misunderstood and rejected. He would then get up, find his sketchbook, doodle a few lines, pretending to draw the woman, then go back to his room to fetch a list of writers with whom he dreamed of working, he said. He made sure to add the name of the visiting woman writer to the list. Knowing they were on 'a list' scared the women. So each one declined his offer. In time, fewer and fewer writers visited the château. Charles continued to produce sketches while thinking about his sister and about June. Today his page is blank. Charles's hand trembles or does not. That's how it is.

§

In the garden, Laure rediscovers a kind of peacefulness. People in the area say roses grow so well here that everyone knows a poem in their honour. In the old days, her mother used to grow them with love, like in the best English films, where the rose has forever been noble. The gardener has mowed the lawn. The smell of fresh grass lodges itself in memory, in that place where the pleasure of living cancels out the throbbing of anguish. The gardener claims he can make grass as silky as a young girl's skin, but he also knows how to multiply the thorns on rosebushes so they can remain forever graceful and entrancing. Behind the cedar hedge, a car is parked: inside, a man waits. He stares at who knows what, but makes note of any gaps in language, any suspension of common sense. Tomorrow a nurse will come to care for her mother for a few days. Laure has spent several nights analyzing the Patriot Act. No verbal sleight has escaped her. She understands the danger this document represents. She hesitates to start writing her report, unsure what tone it should have. The garden is a kingdom. On bright days, one can see clearly the little boats on the lake that, to the villagers, plays the part of a real-life character. Most of the time it is said to be comforting, but on days when nothing is moving, when heat draws the contours of the mountains like in a Caspar David Friedrich painting, movement comes from inside it. Whoever looks at the lake on those days feels threatened to the core.

§

Kim is spending more and more time in front of her computer. One click and Svalbard appears, its amoeba-shaped archipelago; another click and the city of Longyearbyen comes up with its two rows of brightly coloured houses wedged between mountains that are sometimes white, sometimes a soul-wrenching pebble-black. Nary a tree on the horizon of the horizon. On one side, the scar of the old mine, on the other a strange cemetery with tall white crosses that, in summer, form a bouquet of lighthouses in the stone. And then there is Barentsburg, Cape Linne, Ny-Ålesund and Sveagruva, accessible only by plane or by boat. Kim is willing to do anything it takes to survive up there. At first she will work as a cashier in a supermarket. In the following months she will learn to use a weapon, to hike in the mountains for three days, to prepare dog sleds, to dry slices of seal meat; she will study the names of birds, the whole lexicon of ice, the vocabulary of its frightening roar when it tilts and capsizes. The colour of the infinitely turquoise water. The glaciers. Kim imagines the solitude, the cold, the night, the midnight sun. She loses sleep over it.

§

At the château, I occasionally get the urge to drink and smoke, as if that could go hand in hand with the dispro-portionate happiness I experience from savouring beauty and the tenderest nature there is. Tatiana says that this was the undoing of so many writers: this joy, at once minimal-ist and excessive, which, for company, commands impulses that are usually buried but quite active, just as the night is when dawn first glimmers. Such elation at the heart of quietude is dangerous.

§

A diffuse light that makes it possible to see dust particles floods the shop. Behind her counter, June is reviewing some bills. An unknown woman just came in to ask for

Babel. She is staying at the château for a while. She has a strong accent. June asks about the publisher. 'Very well, she is very well,' says the stranger before exiting. Seen from the back, the woman reminds her of Ava Gardner. June phones Kim to invite her to watch *Atanarjuat*, which she just received. This afternoon, she will go downtown to buy *A Woman's Voyage to Spitsbergen* by Léonie d'Aunet. Kim wants to know everything about Svalbard. June provides her with everything she desires.

§

I am calm, though not exactly quiet. The presence of Tatiana Beaujeu Lehmann stimulates my intentions toward silence and dissolution. Sometimes a fierce urge to leave and to not reply to her questions. In this foreign tongue, I'm not quite able to modulate my voice properly, to sort through the tides of desire and the dregs of the essential. I choke on this tongue that nonetheless intrigues me and keeps me alert. In the end, I always find a solution to the questions of meaning that do not come up in my language. I establish links between beings so that I can juggle with their anguish. Every morning, the raw cry of a raven stabs the air, leaving a floating impression of violence and of déjà vu.

§

Yesterday, on my way to pick up a video, I walked by the Hôtel du Nord. The man I had seen at the post office stood smoking, leaning against a tree at the street corner. He seemed surprised to see me, then collected himself and mumbled hullo. I nodded. The irate gaze of a man who appears hurt but isn't keeps me at bay. Tatiana no doubt knows 'the wounded one.' Only in this part of the world do men develop this hunted-animal look, nervous and contemplative. Helped by the wound, some of them display a remarkable gift for seduction and conviviality, but the man before me seemed anxious enough to jolt the day's very heart.

§

She knows her mother's death will soon be a *fait accompli*. In a year, two years. Death will pass through Laure's life for the first time. The body must struggle, for the moment it must boost all its senses to their maximum in order to understand. Let nothing go by. Act as though, but act like so. The bathwater gushes with the steady sound of little falls. All the softness in the world is not found in water. Laure knows the sea can be so untamed that its brutal outbursts are impossible to forget. She puts her hand under the tap to check if the water is too hot, too cold. The transparency, or rather the idea of the transparency, of things, of skin, of her mother's blue eyes – which she has learned to sail through like a threshold, a level crossing, a childhood room – all this transparency makes her weary. The mother waits, seated on a little stool. Laure does not speak. Her back aches from kneeling like this, cut in half by the edge of the bathtub, bent over the noisy bubbling water as if she were crossing a bridge suspended over an abyss. The old mother is now sitting in the tub and Laure is scrubbing. Sometimes her eye falls upon her mother's hands speckled with autumn-hued age spots. Strong hands that can still hold the thick biographies that help dream the time away, help her discover entire lives devoured by the cosmos. Strong hands and ready tears make her mother a fortress, fearless and blameless.

§

I must look after my solitude. Be able to count on it to astonish me, to plot and to go on with this madness for speaking even as I abandon my own language. In all languages, the writer's solitude feeds the little pleasures and great frights of infinite nights. Lives. I am talking about solitude because it is expert at bringing us closer to death, to childhood, to beauty, to nature and even to others, whom it eventually envelops in a precious aura that makes it possible to love them. I have to nurture my solitude. Especially to not let it escape, even though, in the other language, it loses some of its brightness and intensity. Solitude is precious for smoothing out travel's edges: bubbles, tears, secrets glittering in the dark.

§

For years now he has worked wood with his knife, played at carving holes in the blond mass of oaks and of magic charms. He files away curves and smooths, smooths the wood so much so that a composition always emerges in the shape of an armoire or a non-armoire. Yes, an object inside which can be stored a letter, a postcard, a pen, a secret. A beautiful object that is and is not an armoire, that could be a drawer. A safe. His wooden work table is tattooed with inscriptions made by a chisel or a gouge. He likes it when the shape of the armoire-in-progress becomes more definite, when the wood curls up, splits into chips and angel hair. His bedroom is his workshop. To leave the house, Kim must cross the room where the knives are. On the other side of Kim's room is the kitchen. In order to eat, Charles must walk through Kim's room. He always does this slowly, counting his steps and staring either at the floor or at the ceiling, for one day he will want to carve one or the other into a dome, or a tombstone.

§

'We should get together more often before you leave.' June had quickly segued into commenting about the adjective *northern* and the territories in Canada's north. Kim listened distractedly. Yesterday she had celebrated her thirtieth birthday in town and Charles had given her the sketch of a sculpture he would soon make. 'No, not like the cow in Damien Hirst's *Mother and Child*, no, not like the one by Jana Sterbak, no no, something more fictional and more true as well. You'll see.' Charles had always frightened Kim. He knew it, but neither he nor she could figure out where this might have come from. Perhaps the simple fact of still living together as adults made them suspicious of one another, suspiteful of their childhood memories, or melantagonistic, and not at all clever in the face of life. Adding up to a profound malaise inside them that was not at all about to heal.

§

June was more beautiful than ever, Kim noticed. Despite her tiredness, she'd agreed to come watch *Atanarjuat*. They had set up in the small room adjoining the shop. The walls were covered with photographs of actresses and old movie posters. At the foot of the bed, a library composed entirely of books about cinema. June had a passion, Kim not yet. Only this desire for the north. Very far away. For some time now, she had been catching herself murmuring 'before the glaciers,' her belly filling with a kind of euphoria so powerful that she imagined herself at the origins of matter, going forth to meet the light and a clamour of ore and ocean that made everything crack upon its passage. Then images that took her breath away flew off to build their nest of dread and excitement in another part of her brain.

§

Sometimes Charles believes his sketches are flammable. There is always something burning somewhere. Something burning that makes him scream in the night. A book, a movie theatre, a whole village. By day, everything becomes normal again: he goes to the post office, stops in at the café, walks around the château craning his neck, stands smoking in front of the house, sweeps his workshop. Yesterday, in town, people were excited, running, buying no matter what no matter how. Pretending to love each other. At the restaurant, Charles had annoyed Kim with indiscreet questions. She did not answer, he lost patience and insulted her. At the end of the meal, he gave her his blackest sketch. Then they both smoked a lot. Kim wore too much bright red on her lips.

§

In my language, the words *piano* and *writing* are homonyms, and their definitions, nobody knows why, intersect, with a single exception for the zones of silence inherent to one and the other. In the foreign language, *writing* means *to get closer*, while in mine *to have the desire to* predominates. In the evening, sometimes, believing herself alone, the secretary sits at the piano. She plays, stops for five, ten minutes. On the alert, I wait for the melodic shapes of things to come in the château. Her repertoire seems to consist exclusively of Chopin. Once, I came upon her unexpectedly and asked if she liked jazz. Completely transformed, she responded by playing 'Moon Mist.' Later on in the kitchen, we discussed John Cage at length while drinking red wine and eating olives. We enjoyed ourselves and planned to do it again. I spent the rest of the evening immersed in the dictionary. Around midnight, she knocked at my door.

§

The nurse is here. Young, cheerful, without malice. Laure feels relieved. These days of freedom will be precious, yes, she will spend these three days in town, in a hotel room with her books and her computer, working on the text of the Patriot Act. But then, suddenly, a little pain and strong heat come to dwell in her chest again, as they do every time she must leave her mother. No, she has never had the words to speak about her mother. There is no photograph, this is no movie. One can't really know what happened when one entered the world unless one's mother becomes a storyteller of cries, strained muscles and moist eyes, she being the only assigned narrator of the panting, labouring hole of mouth and sex, all of it like a natural order anchored in the mists of time, an otherworldly nighttime that Laure has been trying to visualize ever since she read *The Atrids*. The possibility that there could have been such a night of time, a vast expanse of horizon, voice pitched like the shadows in our steps, frightens her. All the same, she enjoys this dread, which, coming from so far away and so long ago, seems without real danger yet still fertile with emotions and sensations. After making her recommendations to the nurse, Laure leans over to kiss her mother. A strand of wool has escaped from the old soft sweater her mother is wearing. Absent-mindedly, Laure twists it around her finger, a little cord of tenderness.

§

On the train, he reads the newspaper. Nervous. Legs crossed, uncrossed, newspaper folded, newspaper unfolded; cigarette pack taken out of a pocket, turned and turned again, slipped back into the pocket. Charles needs the city. He spent all night sketching. And whenever this happens, the next day he wants to find himself amid traffic noises, senses on high alert, to walk tall among banks, self-serve restaurants, posters, neon, everyday dirt. He is, he says, going to rub up against the city's exciting shapes. After a few hours, these shapes give him ideas and arouse him further, but he does not really know in which direction.

§

Description of the movie. Especially of the sequence where three Inuit women have just gathered eggs. June's left leg is resting lightly on Kim's. Each woman has a handful of nuts in her right hand as though she were about to feed a squirrel, a bird, an eager and faithful animal. On the screen, the scene about death, about capturing the enemy by embracing his soul, is not easy to describe in real time. Particles of time thick with sound come to nestle between Kim and June. Kim's leg quivers. She has put her arm under June's as if they were going hiking in the mountains. Then another arm, a slim waist, another arm, an embrace, a silky hand, another hand, an endlessly smooth horizon. Later on, it's the grave, slow letting-go, the miraculous sinking to the depths of oneself with honey-flavoured words under tongue or suspended between lips. And rippling through the belly, the echo, the clear repercussion of what has cracked, hurtled through each one of the women on the screen. On the sofa, a smell of toasted almonds, sea and peat bog. Kim's body is at the centre of all stories. Kim's life, the only viable script.

§

Tatiana Beaujeu Lehmann refuses to tell her story in the other language. 'Let's speak in our own language, shall we?' Obviously I want to. But as she utters those words while pouring herself a glass of port, I fall into a deep dark hole, as though I've lost my reference points, unable to grab on to now the sounds, now the commonly held meanings of the simplest words. 'I see. Today, you want me to be the one talking. I see.' Pause. 'Would you put an ice cube in this?' White hair in a 1940s style, suntanned skin, high cheekbones, few wrinkles, a slight trembling of the left hand, the publisher recalls the fifty or so persons who, every Monday, used to come to the château to listen to poets. 'After the reading, we served wine in the garden, we also served each other in order to exist. Night would fall. The poets continued to drink and enjoy themselves. No matter their temperament, their inner desert or their tired-ness, they all laughed heartily while punning constantly and quoting other writers. In the same way business people speak in numbers and statistics, the poets quoted frequently, as though quotation were at the heart of their craft, the only practice able to simultaneously attest to their culture, their memory and their mood.' Tatiana believes that poets speak another language but resemble us in that place where beingness falters a moment before it is chased back into the jaws of time. 'They travel, you know, they falter through a very tender darkness that makes them, I've no idea why, transparent. Yes, that's it, light enters them in spite of themselves. Now it's your turn, Anne, tell me about today's world and drop another ice cube in my port if you would.'

§

The lake is always close and far away like childhood. Visible one day, invisible the next. It is the pride and joy of the residents. Children play there until late in the day. Tatiana knows that the lake is a sheet of water, a faithful dog nuzzling for affection yet never giving up the secrets and sweet nothings dumped into it. Since the purchase of the château, two writers have perished there. They say *accident, incident*. Only half the truth is ever told by changing the order of words. The lake is never threatening and makes no waves. It is a sheet-of-light lake. Tatiana has always called it Lake She, the hypnotizing lake that puts the heart to sleep and causes the horizon to rustle.

§

Indiscernible, that's the adjective I was looking for to describe the ponds of meaning strewn without logic throughout the foreign language. Just like at the château, where there is something indiscernible in Tatiana Beaujeu's eyes. It's a word I use to keep from falling into the abyss I've invented for myself. It allows me to all at once better define my fear, compress it and project it into the vast darkness of silence until it changes into a desirable enigma. Before coming here, I did not know that fear was nomadic and that it could be transmitted via vocabulary and characters. Now I know that, in our mother tongues, we have enough words to learn to change ourselves into wolves or sirens, depending on our anxieties, our questions, and this craze for exchanging kisses at the slightest provocation, especially on July evenings when one must make adequate use of one's soul.

Leaves have started falling. The gardener is sweeping up summer's sounds. The roses hold tight in the late August wind. Now the mountains are indiscernible, swallowed up by the eight o'clock fog.

§

Night has fallen without Charles noticing. With its street smells, its victims, its music, that hungry electricity coursing between skin and clothes, from hair to fingertips. Charles will spend the night somewhere, in a bar, a hotel, a park. He will emerge from the shadows at dawn with the new tools he purchased during the day. He says *tools* but somebody will mention the cutting edges of things and one will see billhook, scythe, fauchard, debris, wood chips and sketches all entangled like words in summertime, when crickets and corn, lives and vines, sunflowers and stormy hours touch and quench one another.

§

It's a squeaky-clean city and not at all young. As a teenager she would come here to buy books and visit a friend she cherished above all others, whom she would have loved to love until her body became a passional wave. The city is both foreign and familiar to her, but it will never be foreign enough. Since she had left the area, a slow nighttime had settled into her gaze. She had wanted freedom, chosen to study law as if this would protect her from injustice and lies. She had devoted years to reading law books, believing this would be useful in helping her distinguish between good and evil. The law, she had come to understand, is the necessary conflict of every civilization.

The sight of the great white bridge at the heart of the city always stirs her. She was right to return to the Hôtel Metropole, where she used to stay when she had to visit her mother, unable to spend more than a few hours in her company or to share the late 'Good night, my darling' hour, as well as the early-morning one that tastes of 'It's going to be a beautiful day.'

§

Story of words. All these words in the hopes of making them one's destiny. Have no fear of licking their salt, their origins, the little delights of instinct that catch fire with them. Will we someday have memory enough to recall those centuries when we had nothing but our senses and tormented thoughts with which to face life and turn it into an ally? Will we still know how to recount in what way metaphors allowed us to touch the sky and all the shadows of our fears? That time when we were as fascinated by *hows* and *whys* as by verbs that made us gallop through the cosmos and roll around between proper nouns. Will it be our duty to remember the difficult sentences that nonetheless spurted out of us like bubbles and fireworks? Beautiful torment, beautiful instrument. Who am I becoming in the other tongue? Who translates what in the alternating pattern of words' shadow and desire's infinite renewal?

§

Charles always carries a sketchbook. He slips it into the left pocket of his jacket. He likes the movement he must make to retrieve it, as if he were extracting something from a hunting pouch or a money bag full of fruit. As a child, he loved to draw; then, little by little, he started to strike, to dig into wood. One day somebody said *sculpt* in his presence and he took out his penknife.

He spent the night lying on a bench in the Jardin anglais. He did not sleep. Some youths with radios came very close and did not make fun of him. He did not sleep because of the heat and the flies. He dreamed of shutting them all up in an armoire. Coolness came. When he ran out of words, he fell asleep at last. Now he is returning to the village. He has lost his sketchbook and words have come back, numerous, unusable, like old nails that slip and break. Maybe because of the train's vibration. This train should be stopped. He would like to draw, but without the sketchbook, he can't. His hand trembles. The train is going too fast. Where has the landscape gone? Into the light, of course, that's obvious, he says to himself, into the light is where the nails will fall.

§

I have no doubt: we are often in the front rows of pain trying to comprehend how it is that one day we can take flight and on the next repeatedly bruise ourselves against the world or wander thousands of kilometres away from desire in our labyrinth of images. Discover where the little folds of tenderness come from that, now and again, close up over us like scars, and fire.

§

The hotel room is spacious, with several mirrors that intimidate and make the eye retreat inward. As she enters the room, Laure quickly pretends to see nothing, neither her body nor her thoughts, though they are always tinged with purple. She plugs in her computer at once, places Spinoza's *Ethics* next to the Patriot Act. Orders a salad and a glass of white wine. Does not light a cigarette, does not linger by the window with a view onto the great jet of water rising in the middle of the lake. For a moment she stands in front of the television as if, before getting down to work, she wants to gorge on stupidities and mediocrity; then she sits down at a little Restoration-style desk and plunges into heavy reading about the Carnivore surveil-lance system, which, upon simple request by an attorney from the federal or state government, can be deployed by the FBI. In the schoolyard, the supervisor is pacing in front of the aluminum fence. Laure's mother would pick her up in the car every day when classes ended. She would take her hand and walk her to the red car. Laure would open the window. Her mother would warn her not to throw up.

§

Evenings when it is still hot after dinner, Tatiana, her secretary and I sit in the garden and watch darkness fall over the lake and the mountains. The sky displays astonishing purity. At summer's end there are countless shooting stars. Some of them send out sparks that remain longer upon the retina, creating the impression that we have some power over them if we can see them for more than two seconds. In the distance, owls hoot in the half-light, then all the night's noises come crashing into the conversation. 'In your opinion, how many books were written in this château?' I haven't the slightest idea. 'Three hundred and twenty-eight. You should have seen all the poets. Only during the war years did I see so many worried faces that were, paradoxically, so alive. Several women writers stayed here. I can admit it now, I always did give them preference; but their stories weren't pretty. Oh, not at all, stories so violent that several didn't dare publish them. I did everything I could to convince them, but they were afraid, terribly afraid. Some of their husbands, some of not finding a husband, others of going to hell; others were simply afraid of themselves and of the shame that would befall their family. Things were different back then.' The secretary and I have our doubts about this. Tatiana had done what she could, and I want only to write a book in a foreign language in order to accurately measure the impasses of my own language and not see my own limits.

§

In town the crowd is compact, people in a hurry, eyes ever ready to suck up the future. Trains have multiplied, each traveller rushing with robotic movements to catch his as best he can while thinking of his distress, so minor in today's world. How to shape the stuff of raw emotions into memory? Kim is about to leave. It is now certain: she is going far away. June has promised to accompany her to the airport. First she will film her leaving the house: Kim kissing her brother Charles before climbing into a taxi, Charles waving her off Italian-style, his hand clenched like a child's fist turned toward himself. Kim will film the drive to the train station. The car will drive by the château, then follow the river. Depending on the height of the hills, the lake will appear, disappear. Once at the station, June will get a

close-up of Kim in front of the departures board for neigh-
bouring cities. Then they will get the train to the airport.
June will show people reading their newspapers, constantly
coming back to Kim, her hands, the suitcase. The landscape will speed by. The vineyards, the sunflower fields, the
sheep, the clouds, the mountainside villages: a world
will disappear. At the airport we will see Kim from
behind, heading for the check-in counter, her walk giving
an impression of slow motion, catch a glimpse of the face
of the woman behind the counter, then Kim will turn to
June as if she were about to ask her a question. June will
keep filming Kim's face, her eyebrows, the movement of her
eyelids, the mascara, the moist pupil. She will record everything she can: the boarding pass, the passport, a bottle of
water sticking out of the backpack. Kim will step forward
to kiss her, June offering her cheek while continuing to film,
reframing their close-up faces with one hand. So June will
have filmed a farewell without knowing how to, incapable
of finding a fresh angle, a novel version in which Kim will
have been seen one last time, from behind, never looking
back. At the far end of the image, viewers will make out
customs officers searching travellers' bags. The movie's title
will be *Learning to Leave a Landscape*. Face to the wind, with
the glaciers' unspeakable blue in the background, Kim will
live far away from June, in the all-out immensity that
absorbs sorrow. That's how it is.

§

She has always known how to put her hope to the test. From time to time, the image of the oh-so-blue eyes of her mother lying in bed or shivering in the bathtub comes back to haunt her. This evening, Laure would like to talk to somebody, but nobody in town remembers her. Nor does she remember them, in any case. Her head is filled with nothing but the thousands of pages printed in the name of the Law so that the Law might prevail, infiltrate every dimension of society like carnivorous water, soaking up millions of inkblot citizens. One does not touch the Law without another law authorizing one to do so. A law like Russian nested dolls. Laure always hopes to be able to touch a speck of truth at the bottom of each one of them. But today, why so many mirrors in a simple hotel room? All these facets of the same person, the pain that becomes lighter or heavier depending on whether you are facing yourself or about to turn to face someone else.

§

Evenings when tiredness is too great and allows nostalgia to settle into the château, Tatiana asks me to read to her from a novel by Dostoevsky. She insists I use a silver ritual pointer that belonged to her grandparents. *Yad*. I learned the word one day in Paris when visiting the Musée d'art et d'histoire du judaïsme. Because of its link to reading, I immediately incorporated it into the other language, hoping to ensure its long life. 'Use the *yad*, it will propel me into another world, because, I confess, this one weighs heavily on me.'

I read, the secretary joins us. She does not begrudge me taking her place. She knows that what links me to Tatiana Beaujeu Lehmann is as deep as the lake, which has become an obsessive presence in my story. After the reading, the secretary sits at the piano. An outdated world envelops us and we find ourselves at the mercy of a great feeling of melancholy and fervour. During these sessions, I remain on the alert, amazed at hearing my own voice, husky and multiple, drifting through time, disappearing then re-emerging in me, a foreigner.

FENCES IN BREATHING

Every fly has its shadow.

Châteaubriand

A light at the end of the hallway is I realize quite clearly in the other language a light bulb a thing deep in the eyes that encroaches on words like a symphony in a park on a beautiful July afternoon with traffic noises in the distance and fragments of silence strewn here and there in my life I've been told I should repeat the same words often and not be afraid of burning like money in your pocket and that nobody would complain because the more we are able to catch new expressions in another language the more it becomes legible and beautiful with new sounds so I am going directly to invent the horizon and be careful of my mother's bare feet on the bathroom tiles while my brother waits for me in the kitchen making holes in the hard oak with a knife like he has done ever since he started chasing after words I often caught sight of him naked he was indeed holding his knife in front of him and opening an armoire to retrieve a sketchbook or a message in a white envelope I know I watched him get on tiptoes and he was talking to the armoire singing a tune our mother loved before her death she who all her life wanted to live at the bottom of the lake there to sing while blowing bubbles unable to get to the end of the lyrics while I spread the tablecloth to the vast confines of the universe where reindeer reign as do polar bears always very white when running at the foot of the mountains on the turquoise ice of the glaciers great mirror this I know at the core of my soul although I often remain trapped in the image and the impasse of the violence of glaciers when they start to crack like ice floes I know you have to run and breathe deeply nobody is guilty of breathing well nor of breathing loudly like at the movies or like Charles when he is making his holes in the wooden floor with nails like mouths round and dark awaiting a straw a little pea or a marble or eyes that can see from the inside and that pierce my soul the floor is also a coffin my mother often went dancing there on days when a friend brought cake recipes and Charles ate all the apples yelling Adam Adam it's mine what are we going to devour today the tree or the living wood of the forest while looking at the château in the distance and a lot of words that would love to penetrate me I am not afraid I am not afraid to go where it is necessary to translate the names of sponges and shells birdsongs and the law book that injures if it falls on my fingers are we today going to sponge my mother's large back caress her silences or let them drop into the bathwater while watching the foamy little waves around her thighs and the delicate shadow on her back naturally scrub the spine the nurse had said for there under the skin is a living world I listen to it while scrubbing always a bit harder yet I must finish this report I would like to write what I was told to write without leaving any traces I also think the opposite while caressing my mother's hair as I help her to get up it's as if there were fences in our breathing and this helps me to draw sketches in the morning when I get up and breathing is difficult the sketch is filled with lines and nasty black nails that fall hard on the page if the wind passes through my lungs like I want it to shaking the Damask roses in the garden then I no longer see the fences and can more easily get closer to summer by looking at the lake I love separating the colours and caresses of June and of Kim that estrange me from my soul it's as if I were behind a hedge of thorns when I look at them and I tell myself I must breathe everywhere with my body because I need all of my breath and I also need nails to stash in the armoire for later next to the unstamped white envelope that contains my inventions.

I have secrets that's normal it's true about me as it is about others when I run through my own secrets it's like crossing barbed-wire fences that soil my shirt and make bloodstains on my hands and my knees down to the heels not at all in the morning when there is too much mystery in my crazy canopy bed that I built like a large armoire I pretend I'm breathing or walking while moving away from myself and making sure to scream mysterious syllables that sometimes produce a list of beautiful fruits and vegetables that I put in my jacket pocket then I thrust my hand into the list it's easy to follow with my finger to understand and draw better fences in the end it's true I am on the verge of tears but in a state of fatigue not at all.

People think badly of us because we live in a village with a château vineyards and a post office as landscape and because we hide behind the windows in an armoire in the far reaches of our hearts not at all not at all often I say it's nothing let's give it a good soaping dunk the loofah glove in the water and let's go back to square one to the great cry of dawn let out at birth and then let's dive once again into the tenderness of mothers and let's suckle their breath their breast their life let's suckle from the very first day before going off to wander again estrangement will surely come.

At the château when opening my mail my hands tremble because of age and memory which wrap around the wrists and the beautiful day crouched in my brain like a magic charm deep inside me that makes me tremble with fear they say this often happens when someone is plunged into the void after making mistakes in her language for plunging into the void of one's language and being afraid are similar especially when no sketches remain.

In the morning when looking at the shores of the lake I hold my breath for the roses the shrubs pruned into round shapes the giant trees the wooden floor make me groan as does my mother's great beauty when she is dancing just before falling into the lake with time people have forgotten nobody recalls having seen her leaning over her transparent torment which raised a scorching wind right into my hand and which I was watching closely to see the boats head out with imprints of full-body contact tucked into time yes I love taking the time to imagine how it happened when my mother fell into the lake to finally refresh her hope.

The village is not the village without the flies and their buzzing in the landscape that yields like a great fruit tree a darling of a tree that provides good wood and offers the knife the opportunity to cut into the true shape of secrets not at all it must be said the well-drawn shape of a wounded man for it takes ink or a lead pencil a memory whited-out in real chalk to approach a wounded man one must take pleasure in the true shapes of women enjoying their breakfast while watching the lake in the trembling air that swallows up the light the wind the fog the roses the entire landscape of death and life today my body is restless wild with words and strike-throughs not at all it is just bruised all over like in a dream or when in the early morning I go to the post office to buy white envelopes for my secrets there are strange flavours in my mouth tickly manoeuvres of goldfish or crazy tongues slightly naughty always very soft and full of surprises that make you rush headfirst into the abyss with hands and thoughts flapping so as to hurt yourself not at all because of the strike-throughs in the wood the pieces of bark scattered over the workshop floor I wear myself out making useful holes and looking inside my memory at images of time in the wood it's as if I were opening and closing the pages of a celestial dictionary at will and always falling upon the words *hair fur* and *sex* until a bunch of distant images arise at the same time as June when she kneels in front of me her tongue making little cross-strokes in my full-moon fur my enchanted-lake fur we should do it again so that I too can stroke through June's fur.

In the garden I hear Tatiana's voice repeating beware this beauty is dangerous beware the faces of people who are beautiful heartbreakers beware the holes in darkness that we enjoy photographing believing we are speaking the truth or something important yet it's quite easy to understand that words yield at the slightest opportunity amid birdsongs and clever manoeuvres that do not explain the misery of living beings and the buzzing of flies in ears attentive to the language of humans petals vines and brambles that you wind tightly round stones the shadows of stones and words here I am caught in the trap of words that do not drown out suffering so many cleft words and worried embraces that I no longer know how to make use or hope of so evil and mean has the world become that the day before yesterday church bells started ringing again with a hellish noise that threatens any shaky belief they cover the buzzing of flies the other sounds make no echo in the shade of the lovely afternoon I wait for June's hand to lift my sweater very close to us I hear the steps of a small animal in autumn's new foliage a sound like the rustling of a crumpling page I wait I watch my face still looks for light in the holes of my mother's night the foreign tongue is now in my head daily it crowds me with its words and burns me pressures me with verb tenses that wrap around me searing ribbons sticky tape then it erases me regardless I listen with my muscles and when it's too much I stroke and I strike lather and lather erase whole pages of the book of law while eating my salad.

People think badly of us because I sleep with myself in a canopy bed they're right the bed is ridiculous with its pink silk and apple green which is not a true colour come siesta time it's obvious that beds are full of stories full of murders and blood it's as obvious as scanning the pages of civilization with bonnets turbans bicornes tiaras top hats and baseball caps while always doing whatever runs through your head and a lot of money of course I'm careful I always move forward stealthily and allow myself to roll around in the heat changing my image at every page and every hour I can now rid myself of my own presence change the colour of the night in me change languages to get closer to the secrets on the reverse side of the real oh! how I love to clean the universe with this soft oil behind the characters' backs but we must beware because things stroke things scratch things whistle and hiss immoderately when comes the hour of the bells.

Since this morning I've been wandering through my memory like in a theatre I open and close the curtains I have learned the text by heart I haven't yet had time to think about my makeup when the bells won't stop ringing like wild women they make my text inaudible illegible so then I prefer somebody to play the piano behind my back this way I can hide my feelings I never pretend to be somebody who is wounded like my brother when he shows me his sketchbook my brother I don't know why has left for town with fruit in his jacket pocket why in his hunting pouch he put sketches with my name and June's on them sketches like those he showed me on my birthday and it was frightening.

Nobody can remember everything exactly everything which is why my armoires are empty except when on tiptoes I slip a white envelope into one of them it's not a secret for anyone I slip words into my tiny armoires and have never dared destroy them even though they take up too much space next to the crystal carafes I cannot always pretend that this is happening inside me really for I am me and many others at the same time it is frightening I often go to the hotel to become someone who stretches out next to a woman to sleep in a large room with flowers and a black leather sofa I drink white wine then I get to work while listening to the noises and silences of my damned fellow humans who kill and receive slaves for free without a contract in no time at all it's easy and it makes me want to slip my joy into a black hole when I don't know what to do with my fur I try to remember my pleasures by filing them in chronological order but things of the past are finery and fences too high with their bars they make me feel ashamed they are like a curtain of smooth nails falling on my face all sorts of big scratches that form a grey screen in front of me I prefer hotel rooms with wooden benches already notched and bruised with coarse words like those upon which I sometimes sleep in the summertime I can spend days without speaking to anyone I don't understand why my sister and her friend June look like two madwomen when I speak to them softly and give them my heart.

I often tell myself I've understood it all not at all but what is it I've understood so well I can pretend so well that it's necessary to understand everything I don't exist for nothing my sketchbook is proof of this and I never cry except evenings when I absolutely have to sleep in a park so I don't disturb anyone and because it helps me concentrate on the laughter bursting from all over town women laugh in such ways that we can't see the fences in their breathing and thus I can often touch their fur before going to sleep this morning when I woke up I was myself again I don't understand why I am myself without warning as though since I have been sleeping at the château living in the foreign language has crushed my identity this morning when I got up this morning I truly felt I had reintegrated my movements my breathing my worries authentic and ancient autumn is coming that's how it is coming for sure I am going to be cold and mix up my characters between the lines the number of sketches the naughty pleasures fear and the people I often call *us* I will have to learn to remain in suspense over my sketches to shut my eyes before diving into the blackness when black occurs great big marker of night among the planets I can plainly see that night constantly changes the shade of its jet black and that this is conducive to fear and to the swirling around of words in my mouth when someone talks to me with sincerity in the first person I have trouble breathing as if there were a fine dust of silence and cosmos pouring into me a cannibal force capable of swallowing my own dreams my fictional eyes that so often ache will tell me if it's good or ridiculous to get so carried away into the universe with one's sorrows and one's armoires somebody has spread the rumour that my armoires are antiques I don't want them taken away from me all my envelopes are stuck into the slits glued together with the bark's saliva Kim cannot understand all she thinks about is the north and its ice that reddens lips and cheeks each one of my envelopes has wind in its sails even shut into the back of an armoire I would need mirrors like those in hotel rooms to watch everything that moves for example the silence coming and going from one wall to the other above my head before diving toward me so as to soften my eyes yes I would need other mirrors to face my characters the foreign language deletes my landmarks I am no longer able to describe the village to name the lake and the city deep inside me the horizon is receding we say this about the lines of the hand too yes it's as if my whole body disappears when I read the headlines on the newspapers lying on the shop counter the world inside me becomes more complicated the further I get into editing images yes indeed I lose my bearings it's difficult because of sunsets fading and of Kim leaving soon for sure my shop will be empty and I will be worried due to my good intentions all of this soils my head and damages my sight I so often imagine us heading toward the night.

The world is a huge horse leaning on his shadow with letters all around helping him stand up in the garden or in a child's room the horse carries the child north of the silhouette of the Far North where nobody can see us and where everyone will wait for us in vain once just once in my life I pulled out my sketchbook to see if the horse could gallop between the village and the lake I drew close-ups of his eyes before felling an oak tree in the forest behind June's shop and I made holes and made holes until all shadows had been exhausted then the horse appeared I hugged him close sweat running down my back on my eyelids nobody was afraid of me nor of the horse anymore nobody was really afraid of anything because for once I had made proper holes in the wood without building an armoire.

Talking to oneself doesn't hurt a soul and many people in hotels do it quite naturally talking to oneself is not pretending to talk to someone who is on one's mind or to whom one must repeat insults and sweet nothings like in childhood and the seasons it takes a lot of freedom to talk to oneself about the world we live in freedom is buried I cannot distinguish it under the thousands of pages of law that have come into being since the steel of guns has been firing here and there at the frontiers of the real no one law can be changed without another law authorizing it I enjoy talking alone in front of large mirrors in hotel rooms it helps me juggle the various facets of my body and the objects that decorate the room I am someone who readily acts out of fear that's how it is when I walk three times by the same window that shows close-ups of people's real lives it's as if I were talking out loud to the invisible part of myself so as to not be afraid and so that it gives me joy I rearranged my armoires differently now I can count them there are ten I count only those from after those from before are in the forest scattered among the ferns the slugs and the logs of dead wood the others have little bars similar to crab-fishing cages they are smaller and each one has a white envelope in its centre inside which I do not leave a message this scares me too much like when Kim used to fill spoons with little white mounds and put flour in her nostrils so that her eyes took on these rare reflections that I then had to cross out with strokes in my sketchbook like this |||||||||||||||||||| taking care not to pierce the paper now for sure I'm worried about staying alive next to my sketches it's out of the question to sell my armoires so that strangers can deposit their money and the turquoise blue of their dreamed lives in them.

Stay alive says the voice also applies to all girls whoever you are stay alive because of the smooth wind through the roses and through your raptures stay alive show yourself with your syllables and your images don't be afraid to touch your melancholy stay alive despite the flies and the burns the little decorations everyone's closed armoires stay alive arms open like pages of a dictionary breathe high and loud between the signs the mirrors the little sketches don't forget your grisgris and Latin grammar stay alive despite your mother in her bathtub terrorists and liars stay alive in the moon's axis and touch go ahead touch your mirrors in the right places before watching yourself leave stay alive like somebody who is not you.

What is it in my head that makes me think I am someone else who cannot truly resemble me or maybe the opposite it is frightening this carpet of words the scroll of images and nothing to explain if we are here if we are pretending to be here if we are with someone inside ourselves whom we love or who splits our head in two so that our thoughts scatter deep into the cosmos and that at last we may cry fully emptied of our breathing.

Sometimes I question my mother mere mortal though somehow she shouldn't be using words allowed in the foreign language and not at all necessary in mine where does this taste for immortality come from which always becomes more complicated once one's mother is dead once one has scrubbed and scrubbed her closely with sweet oils and voluptuous silences that always open onto the same landscape with a lake in the middle whose depth is so inconceivable that we need to keep repeating this is no dream to keep reminding ourselves we truly are of woman born and will need to take our time to comprehend all of this and no longer think about fences in breathing.

I always carry with me the clipping from an Oslo newspaper that I have kept since a long-ago March twelve black plastic bags lying side by side on the cement each one containing a human shape stuck to each bag is a rectangular piece of white paper and looking at the limp plastic one sort of gets the idea of garbage needing to be moved if we turn the photograph slightly the twelve black body bags become twelve women wearing niqabs I never talk about death I only know that in life there are fears that simplify meaning and prolong heavy silence.

Today the lizards came out because of the heat their tails glitter like the sharp dazzle of stones soon Kim will be at the seventy-eighth parallel in the land of extreme darkness and of radical whiteness that make the present too vague too vast.

The letters we have traced with the shadows of our arms in order to love somebody need always to be reread I reread I would so like to tell somebody to come visit me even though it's cold in my workshop or in the hotel room where I sometimes go and where there are sofas and large mirrors like those I saw in the château of Tatiana the Russian she who publishes stories of love of wanderlust and of guns I so long for somebody to touch my mouth and my fur in my heart I can now say how one enters someone's thoughts there is love there is no love we settle into it it's that simple we ignite the conversation or not we

take a look around we observe a little now I am pretending to turn my head toward the white bridge to see if
somebody is coming Laure goes by wearing a black suit
and carrying an enormous briefcase she is walking toward
boulevard Long it's easy to describe maybe her mother is
dead I say this because of her clothing I timidly nod she
doesn't see me I don't feel like following her any farther
someone is already following her I will never get used to
time's fluidity in the foreign language it's as if I were in an
eternal present filled with cross-strokes and big fat letters
in colours that are almost images there is little free time for
oneself in a foreign language I always feel confined even
though I am well aware that it is as vast as the imagination
of someone who is afraid of sudden death it is however a
language where one need not be concerned about who is
truly speaking only about the verbs the generic nouns
nothing specific for example to talk about trees and seasons
but hundreds of words to get closer to the stars and so
everybody goes travelling at any time of the year or they
wish to stay in a hotel like the one where Laure and
Charles stay as consolation for living in a village and prob-
ably other things like fences in breathing that I do not wish
to discuss presently one life comes another life goes it's that
simple there up north I will have room to put my hands
everywhere in the landscape shove them right into the
daily gestures of everyone's life I will speak the language of

dogs of polar bears of reindeer and maybe even that strange code spoken by the ugly hairless fox that roams the streets of Longyearbyen I will get close to people they will explain to me how not to fear emptiness while staring into the deep water so clear so cold they will explain how not to die I will have the feeling of being nothing of being infinitely the solitude of infinite silence several roads lead from one village to another one life comes another life goes it is hot in the middle of the sunflower fields under the still-scorching sun of early autumn once in a while a warplane flies over the fields in the next moment we say that each plane is a wound in the azure skies a lion dashing at full speed a pebble thrown with fury.

A great horse with his shadow reappears every time I go to the post office the other day I asked June if she would film my animal and give him life with her digital camera I said she needed to film in fast-forward around the horse while I pulled it in the opposite direction with a thick rope thus we would get a sense of movement the horse would certainly fall but at least we would sense that it was alive June would have to get a close-up of the eyes when I said this my hand was trembling June did not notice but a woman did notice and I felt dizzy with a pain in my chest I did not have the courage to meet the woman's gaze while June was filming my horse I stared at the ground the lizards had not yet left us.

The matters of the other language and of non-sense swirl through the air though I strive to put certain words in parallel I'm unable to make them touch in the right place sometimes a vagueness a slight gap sweeps the sentence away all at once and everything needs doing all over again I'm afraid to run out of words the same way one fears shortages of water gas or food I don't know how to make use of myself in the foreign language I struggle with this and the contour of mountains the pain is more mysterious than ever when I gaze at fields of sunflowers and reeds.

In the lake my mother holds me with arms out-stretched like an offering to the gods I am three years old I can allow myself to be brushed by the soft wind or prepare to fly away by caressing her cheeks and stretching my arms out in front of me like laser beams if I keep doing this a while longer I will swallow a little water and from underneath contemplate a hedge of roses and my mother's face when water penetrates her mouth and nostrils and her breathing seeps away with some red for I dig my fingers too deeply into her waist to hold her close so this is the question who becomes aware of what when we talk about everything and nothing like when I go to the post office or when I hear a fighter plane flying over the village or when I hold an innocuous pebble in my hand I am sad too many shapes are repeated in the unexplained matter that resists me with its shadow its fleeting energy real and illegible I embrace the horse's shadow and this is not good for me I cry only when I embrace the horse's shadow and nobody can see me the sketchbook weighs more and more heavily in my hunting pouch words have begun to make it sink Kim sold two of my armoires and the envelopes inside them then she bought a suitcase I was unable to speak to her to add a word anger is everywhere in my eyes in my hands it is frightening I must buy some nails there is fire in my arms she sold the Armoire of Little Woes and the Armoire of Catastrophes that I had placed behind the black sofa in order to spy between their boards the words of the two madwomen who sit there when I invite them to take tea in my sad workshop.

I had to go to the city centre where the wolves are whom I used to spend time with before knowing June wolves that make holes in their skin their nostrils and their brains the travel agency faces the lake next to the casino I don't know anyone here I would like to not be here I must buy a ticket to go hunting between the glaciers and stop being afraid I must respond to questions by asking questions without mixing up the answers earlier on in the train Laure Ravin who lives with her mother near the château was sitting by a window with her laptop on her knees the screen was bursting with letters she was reading very attentively she often looked out the window her hand was brushing circles on her pant leg as if she were trying to clean it or to remove a stain before disembarking she recognized me and smiled there are clouds I don't like being in town when it's grey June says I will have to get used to the frightening noise made by icebergs when they lose their balance and topple over on themselves she showed me several nineteenth-century drawings of boats engulfed by seas that chill you with dread this is why I suddenly saw the night of time what indeed is the night of time if I am a thousand times the same person in different centuries somebody who has been folded small in the nature of *Homo sapiens*?

The city makes me dizzy with its voices surging out of insignificance and lies it absorbs me in front of the hotel the cars drop people off here and there like pawns there is always a church steeple a labyrinth of words the moving shape of a cloud an indescribable force that destroys strikes brutally while everybody tries to be themselves while I am me sitting at the Café de la Gare drinking lemonade with ice cubes because it is so good for me better even than if I had written all of this while drinking lemonade in a train-station café and had erased it.

People cry easily when tired you just need to look closely to see tears slowly forming then people turn their heads slightly as if to ward off fate I see that their nostrils their chins their foreheads are well and truly alive people act as if nothing is happening and I pretend not to see them getting exhausted from holding back their tears then with a dry and suspicious eye they look straight ahead as if to warn about a coming disaster it's like Tatiana's gold watches glittering in the great glass armoire in the living room on days when this happens I no longer know if time is a light source or a misfortune and I say I must rest everywhere there are power and holes I'm right the power of stars wears me out for example when I lift my head even if it's far it doesn't take much before I feel the heat radiating in my hands troubling black hole this is what I see coming we can't there are things we can't do they happen it is frightening in my head the number of sights that make me want armoires all the more inside which I have to shut a lot of blackness all the blackness I am capable of the purest black ever seen an otherworldly black that attracts like light does by performing very quick magical somersaults something resembling happiness but in the other language this compares to nothing so I go walking alone on the mountain the happiness continues I talk to myself everything is out of focus around what I call the great happiness I must think only of ordinary things because images and words go fast like animals in the forest when they are escaping harm I get excited thinking about everything in life that flees in the name of life.

THE WATER LEVEL

… and met her gaze looking deeply from the same waters …

Louky Bersianik

They were two sentences with water and light. I had imagined them and now I wanted to write them. The sentences were simple, they spoke of unforgettable faces and of a bridge people crossed on foot or in cars. Both mentioned a woman. I no longer knew if it was the same woman in both sentences. One of the women ran her fingers through her hair while the other watched light streaming through the landscape.

The sentences were never exactly the same, depending on whether they were read quickly or slowly. Nonetheless, they always had a reassuring slowness. Wanting to write in our own style two sentences we have just read is natural, just as wanting to imitate someone we love seems quite legitimate and even pleasing. The sentences would stretch out as though they could make grooves in the air or give the impression of a voice and a melody about to drown, one inside the other. The tense changed from one sentence to the other, I could question myself, I could worry. I always felt like starting over. Whenever a sentence skimmed the surface of the lake, characters from a faraway time would spring up, then, without much hesitation, take off into the foreign language to indulge their fiercest fantasies. Screaming was never a solution. Screaming meant a state of emergency. Life needed to be organized to avoid emergencies. Each sentence had her own inner tense and I wanted to settle into it to get a sense of its colour. I had also noticed that, though they had the same number of syllables, one of them took longer to utter. Three syllables did not always equal three syllables. Therein lay a clue that, in each language, time could be stretched or it could contract to make it easier to decipher the cumbersome monotony of dailiness and the tenacious enigma of passions.

I didn't know it yet, but both sentences concerned my most intimate self. 'There must be a reverse side to what I am.' The two sentences spoke about water and about downtown on a sunny day with frisky cumulus clouds.

I borrowed the château's blue Volvo and drove along the serpentine road through Aubonne, then plunged into the forest, taking each curve in such a way as to make my heart race, wild in my chest. Light threaded through the violently green foliage, tropical-summer green. Tatiana had said, 'Go and spend a few days in town, go.' I had listened to her. The road glistened in the sun like young skin. The château, the village, already seemed far off, lost somewhere in the consciousness of an ancient character. I craved the city, craved skirting the shores of the lake and scrutinizing its dark water, happy there was water all around me. Noise, light, everything would do me good. Being by oneself all the time is difficult and perhaps not necessary. We need to be with other people at least half of the time so that life can intrigue, leap and roar. Some days, others are *err and there* strewn inside a story, at other times they are stuck still in the sentences. It's difficult to imagine what comes next. You have to lift your head, breathe.

In my language, I am able to reason properly, to weigh the pros and cons of a hypothesis, to understand my own hesitations, while in the other language, my reasoning is skewed, the slightest ambiguity upsets me and I have no control over the sequence of words. Zones of knowledge have no limits. Reality takes on a vague look. The images I've begun to consider mine become incomprehensible or get stuck here and there in space like disturbing objects, cut off from their symbolic value. Anything can happen, like the other day, when I collided with the matter of evil. A topic I've never stopped to ponder. Everything was unfolding as if this shapeless and powerful thing called evil were accessible to me only in the foreign language, for *me in that language is not me*. Although I am fully aware of how the brain can, in all languages, ennoble evil, restore the senses like one says about a wall about to collapse, set each word like a sharp weapon capable of fixing everything, I can't bring myself to believe that language can so easily deploy inside us not the idea of evil but a theatre of evil. Is there a level of language conducive to expressing evil? Language level, water level. There is always something I don't understand whenever I venture into the history of a city at cocktail hour.

When the two sentences of light and water crossed paths in my thoughts, I felt free without noticing they had interrupted the rapture that had filled me ever since I arrived in the village. I now had a better understanding of what happened following Charles's arrest the very day his sister left for the Svalbard archipelago. The next day's newspapers made a point of specifying that he had been detained only for questioning. Charles returned to the village. He would still stand in front of his workshop, look worried, perseverant, observing the planes coming and going among the clouds, drawing sentences that, without warning, swept both skies and thoughts clean. Neither of the two sentences belonged to Charles. He could hear them. He could see them, but they were not his. He could not put them in an envelope.

It was still sunny when I reached downtown. I parked the car by the train station and headed for the lake. A few clouds were darkening the harbour. Until now, the lake had been but a faraway space, presumably soothing and beneficial. I wanted to be at lake level so as to breathe that mixture of city and powerful water that renews vital energy. I sat near the carousel at the port des Mouettes. Inside her kiosk, an old lady is selling tickets. The facade reads Wetzel Family 1878. With its elephants, swans, horses and little cars depicting the twentieth century's first automobiles, the carousel is picturesque. Three children are at play, preoccupied with driving their vehicles properly in an unknown world where time has no hold. Barely visible in the day's light, dozens of little glimmering lightbulbs girdle the top part of the carousel. I can see Jean-Michel Othoniel's *Boat of Tears*, a work made of wood stripped by salt and the repeated power of imaginary waves upon its sides. The tears, large glass bulbs of blue, pink and yellow, recall the magical glory of light as it might be imagined sparkling in festive garlands above the icy waters of the Atlantic. A night like the Far North and ice floes settles in, majestic and timeless in the afternoon. In the distance, the formidable water jet sprays droplets in the wind, a shower of fine particles of grit with, in the background, the port and its hundreds of white masts and little hulls pitching and rolling in the shimmery light.

Behind me, the Hôtel d'Angleterre calls out as though it has a voice that is grappling with destiny, a voice set to conquer luminous sentences and their swaying above emptiness and death. How to predict where danger is coming from when one is absorbed in a book? Danger revives silences and impulses. How many Hôtels d'Angleterre are scattered here and there throughout nineteenth-century history and colonialist geography? Now a man in a top hat and bouffant pants is staring at me. Behind his barrel organ, he makes the light dance a waltz with the warm weather, then, with bursts of sounds and little rock slides at the bottom of a ravine, he stops everything. Only then does he hold out a bowl. The sun blinds him. Sweat streams down my back. I want a pistachio ice cream because of that tender green reminder of a past life I never mention.

Sentences return, subterranean, sombre, transparent or luminous, as if to make me doubt what it is I see, hear, even desire. Sentences that draw me back to the château and in which I converse with Tatiana, aware of the secretary's footsteps in the hallway, of the dry sound of the piano cover being lifted, then of the first notes of 'Mood Indigo.' All through my head, people are moving forward in time. People are time itself. So is there no true time to master but the one I carry within me?

I ended up heading for the bridge, alert among the crowd of pedestrians and cyclists. The strength of the vibrations created by passing cars surprises me. A woman leans over the parapet. A little farther on, a man smokes and stares at a small grey building called La cité du temps. The man is thickset. I am unable to make out his features. The word *pal* comes to my mind, let's say Al *as in* Alexander, Albert or Allen like the gardener at the château. The water level. From the château, it sometimes seems that the water level is rising dangerously, and when it goes down, depending on the fog, depending on the light at dusk, a new kind of concern sets in. In the morning, the mountain is what first attracts the eye. We know at a glance if the snowy peak is visible. Whenever it is, the fascination of doubt returns: does it really exist, that peak now visible, now imperceptible? The woman has disappeared behind a bus. In the foreign language there are cries I cannot get used to. Cries issuing from as far away as history, slow, funereal, that leave dark traces even inside the mouth of whoever in the distance hears them. Then there are the others: cries that are faster and fiercer, that pounce like ravenous beasts, their energy doubling every time the echo of their own cries encircles them. It's like a game of hide-and-seek with buses poorly framed in the light. The woman appears, disappears, I feel I might know her. The man has moved closer to the woman. First he taps her shoulder twice sharply, then, from the way he fingers the woman's sweater, it's as if he were trying to ascertain the quality of the fabric. The woman pushes him away, stretching out her arm, folding it back, extending it as though trying to find the gesture that will allow her to keep the stranger at bay once and for all. The man gives the impression of wanting to explain something, he might even be wanting to leave with his arm around the woman's waist. A police car stops alongside them. The woman glances toward La cité du temps. The man climbs into the patrol car, head down, shoulders hunched as if he were about to dive into another world. In his head, it's all about staying alive. There are thousands of little holes for shelter. He regrets touching the woman's sweater. Nylon. Nylon. Fall is coming. It will soon be time to dive into the dark.

This is how the verb *to dive* began to take shape. I started saying it out loud, then murmuring it like somebody trying to understand by chanting the same syllables. Diving sometimes resolves the question of diving. Parting the veil, the surface that is obstacle or attraction, opacity or transparency. At the other end of the bridge, while listening to the wind, I felt the verb *to dive* station itself sideways across words and I thought about women's caresses, their hands, the softness of their cheeks, about the slightly crazy heat that rushes to the head and transforms how we see. I wish the lake were the sea, I wish the whiteness of the shore around it would change into milky morning blue, into the soft royal blue of afternoon and the blue again of sea and horizon, as they have been described in my language ever since they became the stuff of dreams. I don't know how much time has passed since the woman reappeared walking toward me. Talking about this passerby in the other language is difficult, and even in my own I can barely find the words, the story of words necessary to appreciate the small and great follies within us of hope, of renewal of energy, and of humanity. Women's caresses are smooth, existential, full of yes, a power of presence and a bond that reaffirms all bonds. Now I am sure I glimpsed that woman in the village. She was wearing a red T-shirt that bared her tanned shoulders. I had seen only one part of her body, the rest had remained hidden behind the tall cedar hedge bordering part of the village. Then I remembered how every time Tatiana recalls an event that is important to her, she says, 'That summer was pure velvet. That was the summer Nathalie Sarraute came to the château.'

I walked on the other shore for a long time and found myself in a little cemetery full of beautiful aged trees under which I stopped. Without realizing it, I found myself at the grave of Jorge Luis Borges. A stone with a two-sentence inscription. I moved closer, convinced I would be able to translate the words that seemed familiar. Nothing happened except that time stretched out whitely as in a Piero Manzoni painting. I knew there was beauty in the inscription, even though there loomed an unspecific threat echoing the fog-laden sentences coming at me at this moment *that's it like at this moment nobody can contradict me because I forget who I am from too much digging in between words, too much diving into the pink and ancient shapes of my love for everything that swirls and sparkles ribbon of slow music that drowns out sorrow in small doses of cello or eyes of a species that shelter a constant sun I've forgotten how the day packs up and goes with tender words crouched behind bare cheval glasses in grand hotel rooms forgotten why in another language I erupt while making a hell of a racket as if this could protect me from the beautiful rolling noise of living beings thrilling in the distance halfway to the half-tremor of dreams. I am everywhere I say I am even though I forget I am waiting comfortably coiled in the roiling of words and of my muscles of silence I am waiting for the centuries to pass. I am everywhere I am.*

Now there is sand, watches, human time and sidereal time in each one of the sentences walking along the lakeshore with me at cocktail hour.

Laure Ravin moved into the Hôtel Metropole hoping, once and for all, to finish with her analysis of the Patriot Act. She has barely slept in the last forty-eight hours, checking, cross-checking the meaning of each word, the consequences of each omission, the word associations that could easily compromise a paragraph, a chapter or a destiny. Her entire body is filled with a kind of anger that seems like a dead end. As though every line of the Patriot Act has fuelled in her a relentless shudder, an indignation, a wild malaise, the precocious intuition that this legislative anomaly will result in her North American humanity plunging into dizzying chaos. The pages of the Patriot Act scroll through her mind with their threatening details, limitations, prescribed sentences, obligations, fines. Every word counts. It can split in two, spill over on itself, provoke a bloodbath. Later on in the evening she will phone home, talk with her mother for a long time, try to reach a civil servant at the Department of Homeland Security to check a few facts. Then, with a glass of white wine in front of her, she will try to convince herself that she is wrong about the extent of this future law's disastrous consequences.

The Patriot Act has become a kind of obsession, a matter of life and death. There is venom in it, programming that threatens certainties fought for long ago. 'And yet my life remains the same,' she thinks to herself. How much time for a looming calamity to materialize? How does our brain reorganize the future so as to erase the mathematics of calamity? How do the voices of the women and men of a country, of a whole continent, harmonize in such a way that it accelerates their sense of being resigned to disaster? The man with the bended knee in the photos flashes by her. He is falling like a mythical statue against a dark backdrop filled with words upon which she had been leaning before she herself fell into the infinite number of physical laws that lighten consciousness.

The room looks over the Jardin anglais and its fountain. Farther on, like a stage setting, are the harbour, the little white lighthouse, the towering water jet. Depending on whether she is sitting at her desk working or standing by the window looking out, she can glimpse either the lake's sky-high jet of water or the garden's tall trees. She has to choose. Impossible to see both simultaneously. Perhaps it's the same with laws. They exist simultaneously, each adding to the others, while we see only one at a time, easy to outwit, or so we believe, and unable to reach out and crush us.

It was darkness that incited Laure Ravin's interest in the law. As a teenager she spent hours in her room reading *The Atrids*, silently and out loud. In the college auditorium, dressed in a white tunic, hair anointed with henna, lips bright blood red, she had been afraid of drowning in a time so remote as to preclude any further imagining of life. A time of chaos, fear and night. She was terrified at the idea of finding herself alone, on the edge of animal madness in the great cosmos of life. She could remain thus for a long time, surrounded by pre-human silence, then the violence of the noises of civilization would grab hold of her again and she had to deal with murders, the blood of sacrifices and massacres, the blood of rapes and births. No corruption. Nothing but blood, clean and clear like life, death, with the sea as background. The sea windless or raging, smashing time itself, so frightening with its Möbius strips spiralling over chasms. The law was a response to this time of chaos. The law was keen, as fine as a blade capable of slicing the pain away from muscles, eyes and faces. The law, in principle, erased fear and kept mothers at bay.

At about six o'clock, Laure Ravin went down to the hotel bar. She picked up a *Herald Tribune* that was lying on a chair and headed for a table in front of the large window looking over the Jardin anglais. The weather had changed, rain was imminent. She liked this Bar du Miroir where, when she was in town, she would come by for cocktails and listen to a Chechen pianist. Each wall was decorated with a huge mirror recalling an Orthodox cross. Seven squares high by seven squares wide. The armchairs and sofas were black or grey leather. The carpet, red. All around, businessmen discussed contracts and good fortune. All had grey hair, as if money protected from baldness.

She was about to sit down when I recognized her. It was the same woman I had glimpsed one day behind the cedar hedge of a nice house in the village. She gave the impression of wanting to talk to me. I was glad to see her. I invited her to sit at my table. She ordered a glass of white wine, noticed I was drinking a martini, like she herself did when in New York. Then she inquired about my life at the château, about Tatiana, whom her mother had known well years ago. I talked about the reasons that had brought me to the château, about my 'relationship to history,' about my sense of estrangement in this village. As though it were very important, she described the vineyards surrounding the château, the tasting rooms where wine always made heads spin and tongues loosen. She spent more time describing a wooden bench behind the church from which one could look at the countryside, see the lake and, on some days, the snow atop the very high mountain. She said she was fascinated by the cohabitation of an ancient world and of cutting-edge technology in each village home.

The sun was setting. The lake was becoming a monochrome presence while its great jet of water, shot through with rainbow colours, switched on like a neon sign. Laure often used the word *lacerated*: lacerated sheets of paper, lacerated painting, lacerated woman, lacerated democracy, lacerated freedom. This epithet no doubt translated a deliberate gesture that suddenly and violently damaged an integrity. I listened to her very closely. I could not quite determine whether I should attribute my close attention to how interesting her ideas were or to what she could represent to me. Out of the blue, Laure Ravin started enthusing about Spinoza, saying she could never refrain from talking about this man whose work she found so contemporary. In the same breath, and at length, she interwove opinion, knowledge and belief. 'Spinoza cut telescope lenses for a living. He was a joyful individual who feared neither exile nor excommunication.' It was obvious Laure wanted to draw me onto political terrain, but every five sentences a word or expression would bring her back to her mother. To hear her talk, one would think I knew her mother.

'My work is composed mostly of reading and interpretation, like in Ismail Kadare's *The Palace of Dreams*.' She was listening to me. She did not know this book. She confessed her ignorance with such fervour that her voice troubled me. The granite table felt smoother and warmer under my palm, the martini transformed familiar sensations into a mini-dose of anxiety and reverie. Outdoors, it was getting gloomy. Could it be that what I was feeling in one language was untranslatable, incomprehensible, in another? *Suddenly everything is so frail from afar from up close to the end of the street we kids loved to play in and with the past and memory demolishing potatoes tasting of ashes and molluscs we loved jumping from up high falling into ravines with words that threw open an abyss in the eyes every time we loved abysses and in their depths what had broken and scattered and needed to be put back into its original shape with one predatory glance in order to keep breathing. As for myself I enjoyed underlining words it was my way to keep repeating in someone's ear if I loved them hated them if I wished them well whenever I underlined I stopped the wind and something would begin that I called grave, deep night.*

Outdoors the weather was changing. Laure Ravin suddenly seemed to want to conclude: 'I must drop by the post office. And make a phone call. Would you join me for dinner? On the other shore?'

They were two sentences at the door of the Hôtel Metropole with a bridge and a touch of dusk penetrating mouths and thoughts. The two sentences touched in a single spot, resulting in a single syllable. Night. In the middle of the bridge spanning the shores, it was a known fact: they were two sentences made to prevent the night from sinking into night. Two sentences sweeping the dark like emergency lights, bright gashes flaring into a fan above the lake.

Laure had bought two large envelopes and some stamps showing the white mass of a bear amid the blue vastness of Arctic glaciers. We crossed the bridge in the opposite direction, lingering because of the beneficial scent of kelp and silt. A slow darkness was descending, slowly sweeping the sky, creating the impression of a field of mist and ruins. At eight-thirty in the evening we made our entrance at the Hôtel d'Angleterre. In the dining room, Laure talked about a frightening world. About the powerful life force that makes us hungrily consume reality and recreate it in imaginary form, dreadfully fascinating and, in a sense, irreproachable. I said I loved people only when they are coiled inside the intelligence of the living. For the lawyer in her, meaning was alive only when brutal and all-consuming. She deemed that reality was but a kind of laundering that made it possible to properly dispose of violence and despair, and that it was necessary to always hold it in the utmost respect, regardless of the emotions running through us. I replied that, on the contrary, it was imperative to dive into the heart of reality in order to thwart lies and the filthy imprints they've left on time like a horizon of culture. We were the only ones speaking French in the room. All around us, German, Japanese, Arabic and English words raised the dust of the present, punctuating diners' laughter and good manners. Between Laure and myself, a life chapter was opening, a discourse of honour gliding word by word into old ideas of freedom and the infinite desire for life.

I decided to walk Laure back to the Metropole. On the way, the perspective shifted. The bridge seemed larger, wider. Behind us the Hôtel d'Angleterre had become just another hotel among the other grand hotels along the quay. The vibrations that were so strong on the bridge during afternoon had ceased. The asphalt glistened under the rain. Car headlights left long red traces. Or white ones, depending on their direction. The city seemed suspended in the playful twinkling of its shores. Ever so smoothly, I had slid into the metaphor of sadness of Jean-Michel Othoniel's illuminated boat. By turning it over to the night, where it belonged, this metaphor seemed even more gorgeous, as precious as the mute tenderness that follows a moment of abandon.

They were two sentences with an idea of time and night. Sentences permeable to death and oblivion. One could readily have believed in a story between them. Each sentence poured its meaning into a great vivarium of torments and questions with words ever easier to caress. Yet each one sought to understand the laws of her own gravity. Whenever the two sentences crossed paths too quickly or too often without apparent explanation, inner reality dealt the universe a sharp, glorious kick. There remained a wound in the middle of the universe. One needed to behold it, then to have no fear of burrowing into it until the universe became the universe again. This is how the sentences moved forward into the night, carrying with them a quaking of the heart, a taste of the eternity that recommences at the edge of the void, as fascinating as dawn in any mother tongue, in any foreign tongue.

Walking over a bridge with someone at night creates a potent moment of intimacy that lifts the soul, one knows not quite why or how, but it always brings us closer to the stars and constellations where it is said that each second exists in close-up, speeds up the continuous flux of perception. Crossing the bridge with Laure Ravin at that time of night gave me pleasure. Pleasure of the eyes watching running water and darkness while the body yielded to vertigo, inconsolable at the idea of abyss and of culture. Walking slowly, letting one's hand run along the wood, steel or iron of the parapet. I'm talking about my favourite bridges, the very short ones, like the Rialto, the Charles iv, the Dragon Bridge. And the very long ones, like the Brooklyn and the Jacques-Cartier. I can see myself strolling through Prague, fists captive to a cold wind that leaves no time for stopping in front of statues of soot and dust, or, in Montréal, crossing the Jacques-Cartier Bridge one June evening amid a singing crowd draped in blue-flag *blues*. All these bridges cast a spell by means of their architecture, their lace crafted from steel and wind, they make us enter and exit history while taking a thousand precautions so we are not overcome by the temptation of elsewhere and of the beyond, which are suddenly reunited in an invitation to cross the threshold of the irreversible.

The Parc des Eaux-Vives darkly stains this city of a thousand streams. The water murmurs from sky to earth, makes everything sparkle in the wind, which is already etching long ripples on the lake, swelling each droplet of the great water jet before opening them one by one like a main sail until the whole thing topples over into the night. Night stretches out, with spots of white suspended suspicious above the lake. Night thick with all the absolutes infused into it over the centuries. It deploys its own peaks of despair and tenderness. It comes apart, mends itself from one peak to the next, penetrates chests where it feeds the sustained fire of births. How to translate what would be our nature in the face of darkness and light? Walking in the night leads to ideas.

At the château, nights are true with, almost every evening, a wide view on thousands of stars, permanent fireworks that Tatiana's voice slowly comments on with silences as flamboyant as those tropical trees that, when in flower, open up a living space in anyone who loves them. 'During the day, most of the poets slept till one in the afternoon. We had to wait till nighttime for passions and impulses to swoop down on fate, all sails set.'

Nuit, notte, noche, Nacht, noc, nit, noite, night in Irish, Bulgarian, Romanian, Macedonian, Arabic, Wolof, *night* in Norwegian, Swedish, Ossetian, Icelandic, Korean, Farsi, Mandarin, Mohawk, Algonquian, Russian, Latvian,

Croatian, Thai, Albanian, Nahuatl, Czech, Tzotzil, Tamil and Cree: night according to the centuries, the eras, night of the Far North where Kim went. Twenty-four-hour night awaiting a full moon that will illuminate the slopes of glaciers, my fear embraced by the cold and vastness. A night of expecting embraces and its feeling of dawn.

'Embraces are like spaces, with wounds or frost, that close upon an image of oneself. I know,' Tatiana would say, 'of no embrace that is fake. All embraces are by definition spontaneous. If ever they become just the muscular result of calculating thoughts, then that day humanity will take its leave, its ancient blood, and flow out of us.' The image of Tatiana uttering these words on a rainy evening kept recurring. There was a wind, like tonight, a wind capable of stirring the cruel and contemporary side of the images in our hearts. Tatiana was talking. I hid between the sentences, ready to pounce or to sink. During the day, I lived in the expansion and edginess of things. At night, I could easily make a synthesis of the world with a kind of softness and well-being that transformed me into a flexible and unhappy being.

In the foreign language, I continue to dig holes and to weave short stories in which I am happy, multiple and worried, perfectly free. Some sensations disappear, leaving dark circles around words. Others originate in the same places. In the other tongue, I uselessly multiply the pronouns, embrace obscurity like some precious object, a small shadow of the big fear.

Laure talked about cities that now have their official *nuit blanche*, one night rich with madness, making people feverish and terribly present. Permission to party all night, wandering among countless shows, holding someone's hand. The idea of having someone to hold by the hand accelerates or slows the life instinct. The hand's warmth is precious. It keeps alive both the singular *I* and the *we* of reverie, without which *intimacy* would be a useless word.

'At the château,' said Tatiana, 'all our nights were *blanches* and filled with words, laughter, poems, gestures of affection, amorous hands. Everything seemed made to help us devour the wind, designed to prolong every sweet little thing fingers encountered: fine fabrics on divans, smooth wood, suede vests, naked shoulders, silk ties, cheeks so youthful, arms so downy. Then all the guests would execute great dives into their dreams, go back to their rooms to perform even higher dives, carving their shadows into the fresh dawn like a rose, something of the self that deserved to be seen coming from as far off as antiquity and the dark crucible of life whence it had sprung.'

We were in the Jardin anglais again. Near its fountain, a group of tourists and bystanders was watching a young woman who, wired to her iPod, was tracing a fiery chore-ography through the night with the help of two round masses at the end of her delicate arms. Gracefully, with her wrists and shoulders, she was inventing a mysterious calligraphy that the wind altered amid smells of oil and sulphur. *Among bystanders there are always the truly inquisitive ones things are so much simpler if we spend the night in a park a little flame glitters as it escapes a plastic lighter it's starting again the characters I put my wounded hand under my armpit Kim is holding the lighter to please me a warm wind brushes her face a Venetian mask scary there is seaweed between her rings, flowers harmful to happiness that is easy to graze on as I gradually move my wounded hand toward her scary eyes that set fire to my workshop.* That's how it is.

Among the bystanders I recognized the woman from the bridge. She had her arm around the waist of a woman her own age. Their converging faces gave off a white glow that answered the fire's ochre brightness. The night suddenly became less night-like. At my side, Laure was lost in thought as though she were moving into a world with its own laws, its commas, its intonations and interpretations. We crossed the street to the Hôtel Metropole.

The two sentences were never-endingly one with the other about everything, a song, a breath, a river, continents, sentences that occupied the body, the emptiness of thoughts, the fulsomeness of living, sentences that plunged into the present and the unknown and, wave after wave, suspended time before heading off again toward eternity, the next sip of wine, a salty snuggle, an appeasement. They were two hungry sentences, one and the same mouth, a carnivorous confrontation between joy and solitude at the heart of darkness that stroked foreheads, thoughts, insults, softened fear, dissolved the salt on foreheads, between thighs, under palms, two sentences that leapt toward faces to glean a little personal history and memory before sliding down into the chest, there to accomplish tasks of hope and of tomorrow. Sentences that did things in grammar and in the wind, did the same things repeatedly as if it were me, in the shape of yesteryear, going back upstream into the time of darkness and the unspeakable.

They were two sentences with wings and desire, one always ready to seduce the other into conceiving, beyond words, a moistness of life in its slightest splitting of sap and saliva, there where the mouth, caressing the dream's fine fabric, ventures all the way to the source.

I could imagine the sentences but I could no longer see myself writing them. In any case, it was impossible to grab them out of the air in full flight or to slow them down enough to grasp their meaning or their scope. The sentences lifted time up like a huge sheet in space and in the same breath took refuge in the slightest nooks of words where, in fits of laughter or spasms of pleasure, they could once again raise themselves in a totally unexpected way so that each one might dream of dreaming still and forever more amid light and darkness.

The sentences generated their own questions, exclamations and imperatives, which, depending on the degree of urgency, always ended up returning thoughts to the body's orbit; face-touching sentences, or shoulder-touching, or touching valiant muscles that willingly let things happen to them. Lusty, merry sentences that could starve or multiply the little sweet rolls, flare into a fan, cause lips to heat up, curve and project themselves into the inexpressible, or coil under tongue with leafy rustlings before reaching unknown shores. Most of all they were night-wandering sentences that reminded me of the vertigo of long-gone days, sentences with honey, with rice, with fragrant oils and death *in absentia*; it was an intoxication of lips and the flavour of flanks, every time thirst touched a verb, there was in each sentence a cloud or a storm that increased the rhythm of breathing, they were good sentences, senselessly good, eternal, ephemeral, arousing mucous membranes and taste buds.

Tomorrow I would go back to the château and once again immerse myself in the complex world of Tatiana Beaujeu Lehmann and the everyday life of an archaic and global village. The foreign language would continue to flourish and to transform me. I would shelter it for a time, then, suddenly, it would be chased from my thoughts.

The early-morning light was about to melt into the great gleaming jet of water. A first crack of dawn wet with serenity. A quiet moment before Beirut, in flames, sinks into the middle of the lake and of the reconstituted present.

LEARNING TO LEAVE A LANDSCAPE

And we, spectators always, everywhere,
turned toward the world of objects, never outward.
It fills us. We arrange it. It breaks down.
We rearrange it, then break down ourselves.

Rainer Maria Rilke

Autumn. I watch the movement of leaves at the top of a
tall tree, always the same one in my gaze ever since I came
to the château. I slow the speed of word after word so that
Tatiana can, with calm and serenity, enter the realm of the
gentle time that is no longer euphoria but an endless dawn
with its own heat. The château has been turned into a
museum. On display are Charles's armoires and sketches,
June's photos, and albums of letters and dedications
collected from poets who stayed at the château. Part of the
living room is now a screening room. Twice a day, one of
June's films is shown, one of those she made while she was
living with Kim in Svalbard. The two of them now take
turns looking after the library and the archives. Part of

what was once the large room with the canopy bed has become a surveillance centre. Five cameras have been installed to protect the château, to which more and more people have access.

Tatiana was quick to understand that the landscape no longer belonged to us. She was slowly preparing to leave, gradually forgetting the details that make one smile, or cry, or want to go for a walk along the chemin du Signal to contemplate the lake and the city. I too was beginning to feel a lack of landscape. It was eluding my thoughts and desires. I would not be able to keep talking much longer about this setting that we would soon leave.

Our pleasures, our fears, our conversations, everything that gave us a sense we were living intensely, all this was about to be neutralized, changed into invisible strips of ribbon spiralling above our lives. Ancient languages were translated less and less frequently, as though they had become unfit to reflect the world. Everywhere, egos tossed and turned counter-clockwise. The nature of time itself was changing. That's how it is.

Nobody understands anything anymore about events that a mere five years ago were considered commonplace and familiar. On this side of the lake, everything is changing through little tasks, details and regulations. Catching up with one's life has gradually become impossible, for life seeps out from everywhere, carrying away the presence of each one of us. Nobody understands a thing other than that life gives the impression of not having changed one bit, of being, oh and yet, oh and how, already other, and of continuing its metamorphosis.

We no longer set angry feelings on fire: they die out on their own, slowly, like the wind. One day anxiety grips us, the next day things are different; all it takes is a little light rain that makes you want to cocoon, to crawl deep into the ancient language, but then one day anxiety returns and we wait for words to spill from our throats, unpronounceable and rubbery. With time, we hope their nameless opacity will make us want to rebel.

I now sleep in the library, I mean in a small room adjacent to it. A bed, a chair, that's all. At dawn, I can't tell if I'm in my room or in the library. I'd like to experience strong, spirited feelings that would leave me in a perfect state of hope and creativity. In the other language, I was an animal sated with hoping and instinct, carnivorous and chameleon. An animal with sharp hearing who, from very far away, could hear the cries and sounds of the wind while immensity lay curled up inside me. I would circulate between pronouns then wait for somebody to start crying or for tenderness to join with dew. I dwelled in my hunger. I always went further.

Today, I am clinging to the landscape. I am trying to hold it back with my body of silence. Waiting for sensitive things and shapes to awaken in me the ideas necessary to comprehend the world. There is a way of being on the alert and letting our senses do the work. We sometimes have to think, but I've noticed that we do it only when forced to, either to solve a problem or to prepare an answer. Choosing is increasingly difficult. I prefer daydreaming, especially in autumn. Not everything can be explained: the crises arising from the inside, the others we see coming that appear like bouquets of images outside the self.

I drink a lot of coffee. At breakfast I eat pasta with a bit of olive oil and cayenne pepper. I slip into the daily life of the château, slyly longing to write another book, in my own language this time. Laure Ravin is in town. Now and then she drops by the château for cocktails. For years, she and I commuted between New York and Montréal in order to keep on loving one another. Over a forty-eight-hour period, we would celebrate a new time with its own infinite clock ticking. This lasted until border crossings became longer and harder. When war broke out between our two countries, we stopped seeing one another.

The museum is open Tuesday to Thursday from ten a.m. to three p.m. On the other days, the château is used for receptions held by multinationals with headquarters in the city. Today the château's foundation is welcoming a Chinese group representing the oXcimore company, a big champagne producer. There are about thirty of them.

Several without wives. The terrace buzzes with the tos-and-fros of tones rising, falling, neutral like exclamations and waterslides amid birdsong.

The water level has gone down considerably. It's as if the lake were leaking out the bottom. The city has had to stop piping water to the great jet. From the château, the lake is a still, sombre mass. You now have to pay admission to walk in the Jardin anglais, where several murders have been committed in the past five years. Three times, young immigrant women who did not speak the native language, burned alive. You have to pay admission. That's how it is.

There is only one newspaper left in the area. Charles publishes sketches in it three times a week. He rarely comes to the village now that he lives in town. From time to time, someone invites him to a reception. He walks by his old workshop. The smell of fire still hangs in the air after two years. There is nothing left but the foundations, scattered stones, beautiful, among which crawl insects and weird little beasts. At the château, during the receptions, he sketches portraits on request. They're well done, soon done. The rest of the time he talks with the wives. He tells about how in the old days he spent hours sitting in this very garden with great writers discussing Spinoza and Nietzsche as they drank and smoked till dawn. Writers who had no fear. He smiles like a wounded man with tenderness in his eyes. Sometimes his hand trembles alongside his body. That's how it is.

I published a first book written in the foreign language, which I speak more and more frequently and in which I am even able to express with precision feelings I am experiencing for the first time. For example, I succeeded in translating what happens when a piece of oneself breaks free with a loud noise or goes softly away toward an *ah! so far away!* that is nothing like a horizon. Sometimes I try to imagine what June and Kim feel for one another. I still occasionally write in my mother tongue, mostly when sitting in the garden or after a conversation with Tatiana. Our conversations now unfold slowly, as if we were constantly bathing in an Italian afternoon along the Adriatic. I need sounds like the song of cicadas or crickets in order for childhood words to resurface. That I will say, although I experience fewer and fewer emotions. Yes, when someone cries. I have a sensitive ear and react to the slightest change in breathing, tone, volume. I know if it's coming from the glottis, the nasal passages or through the whole chest.

The smell of ink lingers in the landscape. I am trying to understand. Inside/outside. What is inside me? What is outside and why should this matter if it is not in me? Having a body is something we rarely think about because it is normal to be in one's body and to follow it like an instinct that precedes our thoughts. Having a body comes from the verb *to be born*, and the word *mother* is never far behind. The body of she who gives birth varies very little from one language to another. Later on, we see if there is tenderness in her gestures, if the tenderness is repeated.

When the sentences in my head became shorter, tighter, I understood that I could at any moment fall into a disturbance of the senses, get violently carried away in mid-sentence or lose all sense of time in that same spot. It's one of the reasons I cling to the landscape like a surreal little girl in the centre of a drawing of a beautiful blue sky with a shimmering horizon.

Around the château, it's like there's nothing left but the lovely smell of roses and cedar hedge. Al, the gardener, still works here. He comes twice a week to rake, weed, water, harvest. With him I can talk about the war. Nobody around us wants to discuss it. It's a taboo subject, just like what happened in Montréal in December 1989. He is very familiar with the geography of both countries. He knows all about the trees and plants from the very tip of Key West to the shores of Baffin Island and even farther north. Hibiscus or potentilla, palmaceae or betulaceae, he knows. I can tell him how I went from Montréal to Gaspésie, then on to Halifax, where there were still boats that met up with ships in international waters. One day he simply said, 'Water, I pushed their heads under water. It could go on for hours. You couldn't make a mistake and keep the head under too long. It was horrible. There was always a risk of breaking their necks, we had to work in twos and be gentle with our big hands. That took good judgment. The palms of my hands can still feel the slippery scalps, the wet hair getting tangled between our fingers. Their heads thrashed about vigorously. The faster they moved their heads, the more noisily they suffocated. It took patience. We always played music *made in U.S.A.'* I now believe there is something unreal in this man. I can no longer look at his hands. He said he wanted to leave for Thailand soon.

More and more I love darkness for itself, it soothes me, makes me feel good, though I don't quite understand why. I also love it because I am trying to imagine language without light, as though I wanted to understand how things were before language, when, deep in the throat, syllables and vowels were not yet organized and it was necessary to tilt one's head back to allow sounds to fly through the open air, terrifying, guttural or strident. In the beginning, I thought the other language would enlighten me, clarify the mysteries of my inner life. I wanted to learn to read inside myself. Reading inside oneself may not be important.

Somehow, by setting the original *me* and a fictional *me* in a foreign language, I thought I might succeed in covering every angle of the idea that the body renews itself. I rarely write in the 'desperately tomorrow' mode, yet it does happen, such as right now, when the voice, in fragmenting meaning, becomes concerned, oh and how!, with seeing itself go thus with its hand outstretched toward infinity, in life and in death. I then grasp that if this irresistible arousal requires words, it's because their great reserve of the absolute revives the meaning of life time and again. Meanwhile there will be, there were, hollows, games, depositions. What is there to understand other than simple sentences like those I read sitting in the garden in the afternoon, craving images? What else is there to read but my intention to not disappear?

At the time I was writing the book in the foreign language, I had come to believe that the effort required would be so great that it would force me to refine the meaning of what I nonchalantly called my 'desire for immensity.' I knew the foreign language had the reputation of containing a large number of words used to measure and interpret the physical world. Words abounded to talk about the cosmos, black holes, dark matter and constellations. What's more, this other tongue allowed me to shift from I to third-person singular and vice versa without justification, without crossing the bridge of identities and differences. It was useful to me from dawn till dusk and always gave me the impression of standing in the truth of things and of sensations. With this language, I was simultaneously intimate and public. I was afraid of nothing. I claimed to be afraid of nothing, for I could also lie whenever it struck my fancy. To enter and exit at will the landscape of my loves and of my anxieties.

Inside/outside rolls the language of passions. Part of me is visible, the other sunk into the invisible. Every hour imperceptibly shifts the visible part of what I am into another dimension. The invisible part whirls around the garden above the lake, I know it sometimes goes back to the darkness of before language. This I know. It's the invisible part that gives life to the life in me and around me. I would like to know what it is made of and how it travels through the body without ever quite rendering it nostalgic.

A few moments ago, we saw an aurora borealis, a phenomenon quite rare if not impossible at this latitude. Yet there it was, flaunting its curves, its breathing, its all-powerful choreography of arabesques. Tatiana leaned over to me: 'You can see, can't you, that time is visible. Just look at those watches in the armoire. The time you spend watching time makes it visible. Surely you're aware that time is a great curved horizon that barely separates us from our origins.' It was at that moment that the first curves of the aurora borealis appeared. Kim and June joined us with piping-hot tea, which we sipped slowly. The sound of the cups being put down onto saucers, the movement of the little spoons tapping against the edge of the china, nicked the silence. It was still possible for our dazzled eyes to embrace the blackness of northern-hemisphere nights.

Every day now, in my mind, I am sitting in the garden imagining the present. As though it were my true nature,

I am starting to want to touch the invisible part of myself. I am tenacious in the landscape. I would love to be able to give darkness a new name.

The war is still raging over the Northwest Passage. I am everywhere I am. I don't dare write: I am frozen, fossilized in combat position.

NOTES

The epigraphs are from the following publications:

Page 7: Alessandro Baricco, translated by Alastair McEwen, *Ocean Sea* (New York: Knopf, 1999).

Page 11: Joë Bousquet, *Le meneur de lune* (Paris: Albin Michel, 1946/1998). Quote translated by Susanne de Lotbinière-Harwood.

Page 51: François-René de Châteaubriand, *Mémoires d'outre-tombe* (Paris: Penaud Frères éditeurs, 1849). Quote translated by Susanne de Lotbinière-Harwood.

Page 73: Louky Bersianik, *Axes et eau, poèmes de « la Bonne Chanson »* (Montréal: VLB éditeur, 1984). Quote translated by Susanne de Lotbinière-Harwood.

Page 103: Rainer Maria Rilke, translated by Stephen Mitchell, 'The Eighth Elegy,' *The Duino Elegies* in The Selected Poetry of Rainer Maria Rilke (New York: Vintage, 1982).

ACKNOWLEDGEMENTS

Nicole Brossard thanks the Foundation Ledig-Rowohlt for the three weeks spent writing in Le Château de Lavigny.

Susanne de Lotbinière-Harwood warmly thanks the Canada Council for the Arts for making this adventure possible through their financial support. Also, big big thanks to Alana Wilcox for her unfailing editorial presence and brilliant attention to detail. And of course, to Nicole Brossard for trusting me, once again, with what matters.

ABOUT THE AUTHOR

Nicole Brossard was born in Montreal in 1943. Since 1965, she has published more than thirty books, including *Museum of Bone and Water*, *The Aerial Letter* and *Mauve Desert*. Her contribution and influence to Quebec and francophone poetry is major. Brossard has twice been awarded the Governor General's Award for Poetry, first in 1974 and again ten years later. In 1965, she co-founded the literary periodical *La barre du jour* and, in 1976, the feminist journal *Les têtes de pioche*. That same year, she co-directed the movie *Some American Feminists*. She was also awarded the Prix Athanase-David, Quebec's highest literary distinction. In 2006, she won the Canada Council's prestigious Molson Prize for lifetime achievement. Most of her books have been translated into English and Spanish and many others in different languages. Her collection *Notebook of Roses and Civilization* was shortlisted for the 2008 Griffin Poetry Prize. Her most recent book is an anthology of her work edited by Louise Forsyth, *Mobility of Light*. Nicole Brossard lives in Montreal.

Susanne de Lotbinière-Harwood lives in Montréal, her home-town. She is the auther of *Re-belle et infidèle: la traduction comme pratique de ré-écriture au féminin / The Body Bilingual : translation as a rewriting in the feminine* (Remue-ménage/Women's Press, 1991), and of many texts about her practice of both literary and art text translation. As a translator she has co-authered numerous works of theory and fiction, into English and into French, and was shortlisted for the Governor-General's Award in 2005. Her practice has led to parallel art experiences, such as years of "performative lecturing" in North America and Europe, and an exhibition of her art text *translation artefacts* (Galerie La Centrale/Powerhouse, Montréal, 2001). After teaching for two decades, she is now figuring out what being retired means. This is her fourth Nicole Brossard book.

Typeset in Jenson
Printed and bound at the Coach House on bpNichol Lane, 2009

Translated by Susanne de Lotbinière-Harwood
Edited and designed by Alana Wilcox
Cover image, *Ellipsis 01*, by Christine Davis, courtesy of the
        artist and the Olga Korper Gallery

Coach House Books
401 Huron St. on bpNichol Lane
Toronto, Ontario M5S 2G5

416 979 2217
800 367 6360

mail@chbooks.com
www.chbooks.com